Fox Farm

Eileen Dunlop

Fox Farm

Holt, Rinehart and Winston / New York

Printed in the United States of America

10 9 8 7 6 5 4 3 2 1

Library of Congress Cataloging in Publication Data

Dunlop, Eileen.   Fox farm.

   SUMMARY: Through caring for a stray fox cub, a ten-year-
old gradually accepts the fact that, though he too has
been abandoned, he does have a place in his foster family.
    [1. Foster home care — Fiction.   2. Foxes — Fiction.
3. Scotland — Fiction]   I. Dinsdale, Mary.   II. Title.
PZ7.D9214Fo   1979   [Fic]   78-14091   ISBN 0-03-049051-0

For Hilary and Dema Sagovsky

Contents

Mr. Darke shot the fox on a night in early March, when there was frost in the air, and the moon and stars shone with bright edges in the inky sky. She was a clever old vixen, with sharp ears and eyes, and she had been avoiding traps and giving human enemies the slip for years, but now her time was up. The boys, lying awake in bed, had been waiting for the shot, not on that night only, but every night for weeks, ever since the first attack on the henhouse, with its morning horror of torn feathers and blood. But even so, when it came, sudden and short, without reverberation, the shock was terrible, the leap of the heart, the tightening of the throat, the spasm of movement which shook the bunk beds, the spontaneous feeling of pity and regret.

Silently they slipped out of bed, and crossed the linoleum on bare, curling feet to the window, parting the thin curtains to peer out into the coldly-lit, sharp-shadowed night. The birds, who had risen with a loud flurry of alarm from the thicket between the house and the river, had decided that after all the shot had nothing to do with them, and were settling back crossly on to their perches; otherwise, nothing stirred. The leafless apple trees in the orchard were like charcoal drawings of trees, dense and velvety, against a navy blue paper sky; the image of the full moon broke into a thousand fragments on the quietly rippling river. There was no intimation that death had come suddenly to a free, wild thing.

Then, below the bedroom window, light fanned out, and steadied into a rectangle on the cobbled yard, as someone opened the back door; craning their necks, the boys saw

Father come round the corner of the house, big and bulky in his duffle coat, dragging a dark burden. He dropped it out of their line of vision, at the corner of the doorstep, and went into the kitchen. The light on the cobbles disappeared, and without speaking, the boys went back to bed.

Nor did they say anything in the morning, when they stepped out into the grey dawn to feed the hens, and carry pails of swill to the pigsty, and saw the vixen stretched out in the yard, cold and stiff from her black nose to the delicate tip of her brush. A grey film had formed over her eyes, and her teeth were bared in a frozen yelp of fear; there was something pitiful about the dead fur covered with rime, and the dark blood congealed around the small, neat hole in her breast. They hated to see the poor creature lying there, exposed and undignified.

But when they came back to breakfast, they saw that Father and David had already carried it away.

I *An Orphan*

It was Friday night when the fox died, and at three o'clock the following afternoon Richard and Adam were coming home from the school at Garlet, where Adam had been playing in a football match, and Richard had been watching him. They had a journey of two miles, down the steep hill from the village and across the wintry plain which separated it from the river, and the croft on its bank where they both lived. They could see the croft, never very far away, with its huddle of reddish roofs and grey chimneys crested by a row of tossing poplars, but it took a long time to reach it because of the casual nature of the road, which wandered hedgeless and ditchless from house to house, and only got to Fox Farm by accident, or so it seemed.

The boys had only one bicycle between them; it really belonged to Richard, but he shared it, like everything else, with Adam. They took turns scrupulously, Richard from the school gate to the cottages at the foot of Garlet Hill, Adam from the cottages to the gates of Fourwells Farm, Richard as far as the backward-pointing fingerpost which said, *Garlet 2 miles*, and Adam from there to the stunted, cactus-like tree at the end of the croft road, where Richard's father had hopefully nailed up a painted board announcing:

R. and M. DARKE

EGGS POTATOES PLANTS AND

GARDEN PRODUCE IN SEASON

Richard was usually permitted to ride the bicycle from there, since Adam was too lazy to take it all the way down to the stable, and walk back to the house. They might, Richard knew, have had a different kind of sharing; if they had been really friendly, they might have gone on the bicycle together, taking turns at pedalling, for they were about the same size. But as things were between them, this ride-a-while, walk-a-while sharing was better; the rider soon out-distanced the walker, and there was no need to talk.

Richard was walking now, trudging with hunched shoulders and hands thrust deep into his pockets, along the last stretch of road, between the fingerpost and the notice-board tree. The weather had changed since their departure three hours earlier; grey clouds had marched up from the other side of the river and a damp, blustering wind had blown away the rime which had stiffened the coat of the unburied fox, and furred the dry earth and grass along the margins of the road. There was usually a wind blowing down across the plain from the hills to the river, for there was nothing to break its onslaught; it simply divided on either side of isolated barns, farmhouses and haystacks, and only a few gnarled, hunchbacked trees persisted in putting down roots in such hostile places. The wind blew down Richard's collar, and made his thick hair stand up like brown grass all over his head. There was a smirr of rain in the air.

Ahead of him, Richard could see Adam on the bicycle, his red head the only dot of bright colour in the landscape. He was weaving slowly from one side of the deserted road to the other, driving the front wheel through the ruts made by the farm carts and lorries, wobbling crazily to and fro. Richard watched him in silent exasperation which was mainly directed against himself.

Why, he asked himself, not for the first time, did he still insist on behaving as if he and Adam were really friends? Why, when he might have spent the day in his room, making up a model of *Apollo IV*, or reading *Seven Years Before the Mast* by the kitchen fire, was he tramping along this boringly familiar road, having spent his precious free time watching a boring school football match, all for the sake of someone who did not in the least care whether he did, or not? For Adam didn't care: he would have slung his football boots round his neck, and have gone off quite happily on Richard's bicycle, and would not even have bothered to tell him the score when he came back.

Richard asked himself this kind of question often, without reaching any very satisfactory conclusion. He had long ago given up the hope that he and Adam would ever be more than acquaintances who shared a room; such dreams as he had once had of real brotherhood with Adam had been shattered within a few weeks of Adam's arrival at Fox Farm. Adam had come because Richard's mother had heard a social worker give a talk at her Church Mothers' Group about the need for foster-parents for homeless children; she had come home much in favour of the idea, and, being an eloquent woman when roused, had lost no time in persuading her husband and children that they must make room in the family for a foster-child, with a view perhaps to adopting him, without delay. So Adam, thin, red-haired and watchful, had come; he had made no trouble, but equally he had made it plain that he was only passing through Fox Farm, as he had passed through many places before. He went to school with Richard, and shared his chores, and slept in a bunk bed in Richard's room, but he kept his suitcase under the bed, handy for the next move. He liked nothing that Richard liked; he never read a book, or drew a picture, or constructed a model, and without actually saying much, he managed to make his low opinion of these activities clear. Yet still Richard went on sharing his belongings with him, helping him with his homework when he got stuck, which was often, and going to cheer him on whenever he played in the school football team. But he was never sure whether he did these things because he felt sorry for Adam, or because, in spite of everything, deep down inside himself he couldn't help liking him.

Today, the atmosphere was a little more tense than usual. The boys had not mentioned the shooting of the fox, because they shared everything except their thoughts, but all day the image of the frosty dead beast with a soundless cry at its mouth had been coming repeatedly in front of their eyes, when they were actually looking at quite different things. Richard could tell that Adam disapproved whole-heartedly of the killing; he had seen it in his face when he came out into the yard before breakfast. But it was an easy matter for Adam to take the fox's side. They were not his hens which had been hideously slaughtered, not once, but three times, nor was it his father who toiled fourteen hours a day, summer and winter, to wring a decent living for his family from four fields, a tiny orchard, a henhouse and a pigsty. And didn't think he could make it through another year, Richard remembered, with a little squeezing of fear in his chest. He too hated the death, the violent end of a creature which had, after all, only been fulfilling its nature, but he had other loyalties. It was not so simple for him to make a judgement in the fox's favour.

Adam had now reached the notice-board tree. From several fields away, Richard could see the bicycle propped against the trunk, and Adam sitting on the grass verge, waiting for him to catch up. It happened every time; when Richard did eventually reach him, Adam would be lolling indolently against the gate-post, shying stones at the telegraph pole on the other side of the road. He would continue with great concentration, applauding himself quietly at every hit, till Richard had taken the bicycle, and ridden it off down the rutted lane to the croft yard. Then he would leisurely get to his feet, and wander down to the kitchen, to warm himself by the fire.

Usually, Richard accepted this, like much else that was unfair, without a fuss, but today he was on edge; he was cold and damp, and angry because he felt that Adam was silently putting him in the wrong about the fox.

'I'll give you two minutes to take that bike down the lane,' he muttered between his teeth as he rounded the last curve in the road, 'then I'm going to tell you exactly what I think about that, and a whole lot of other things.'

And for once, he meant it. But when he had caught up with Adam, he discovered that something had already happened to break the usual pattern of events.

For Adam was not throwing stones at the telegraph pole; there was not the usual regular, muted cracking as each one bounced off the dull wood and fell into the long grass below. Instead, he was sitting perfectly still, holding some lumpy object inside his jacket, and it was absorbing all his attention, for his chin was down on his chest, and he was peering down his own front with a concentration which Richard found faintly comical.

'What have you got, then?' he asked, flopping down beside the other boy in the wet grass.

Adam did not reply. He raised his head, and looked at Richard with his alert, faintly accusing blue eyes. Then he pushed back the flap of his waterproof jerkin, and to his astonishment Richard saw a face looking out between the lining and Adam's jersey, a little brown pointed face with golden eyes and a faintly snuffling nose.

'It's a puppy,' he said.

'It's a fox,' Adam said clearly, in a tone which invited no argument.

A moment passed before the full meaning of these words sank into Richard's consciousness, and the force of the accusation made itself felt. Then, in spite of Adam's dogmatic manner of speaking, he wanted to argue, to disprove what he said.

'You can't know that,' he said, trying to sound firm, and hearing himself sounding feeble. 'I mean, you can't know for sure.'

Adam looked contemptuous.

'I know a fox's face when I see one,' he replied curtly.

Richard stared intently at the prick-eared little face peeping out from Adam's chest, and he had to admit that it looked very like a fox.

'Where did you find it?' he asked.

'Just here, see, in the long grass behind the tree. I sat down to wait for you, same as usual, and I heard something rustling and snuffling about. It was crying with cold—it's still shivering, poor little thing.'

Again the note of personal accusation. Richard winced.

'How do you suppose it got there?' he wanted to know.

Adam shrugged his thin shoulders, but he had an answer for everything.

'I suppose,' he said, 'when it realized its mother wasn't coming back, it ventured out to look for food. The lair must be over there somewhere'—he waved his hand vaguely in the direction of the low, scrubby wood which bounded the croft on the south and east—'not very far off. It's probably starving,' he added, watching Richard to see how he would react. Yet when he saw Richard's brown face looking bleak and stricken, he felt remorse, secretly. 'Do you think we could get him something to eat?' he asked, less coldly.

It was a relief beyond measure to Richard, who had been feeling like a prisoner in the dock, to be asked for practical help. He scrambled quickly to his feet, saying eagerly, 'Yes, of course we could. Let's take him into the kitchen. Mother and Dad won't be back from Millkennet before six, because this is the first Saturday in the month, when they always go to the Queen's Hotel for tea, and David is staying the night with Angus. So we'll have the place to ourselves for a bit. We can get the fox warm by the fire, and I'll pinch some mince for him out of the freezer. Hey, listen, Adam—you're sure it's a him, aren't you?'

'Yes. I checked,' said Adam. 'Have you got the key?'

'No. It's under the flower pot beside the back door,' replied Richard, mounting the bicycle and riding away.

It was quite a long walk back from the stables, where the Darkes kept the van and the bicycles and the farm equipment, for they had no horses. When Richard reached the kitchen, he found that Adam had already made the little foxy creature comfortable before the kitchen fire, on one of Mrs. Darke's best blankets, which he had removed from the laundry basket. Richard feared an accident of a kind which would be difficult to explain, but did not like to make a fuss when, as far as Adam was concerned, he was already under a cloud of disapproval. So he said nothing, but took off his coat, and came and squatted down beside Adam on the hearth rug, looking at the animal now revealed to him in its entirety for the first time.

It was a little rusty-coloured beast with a longish, thin body and spindly legs; its face had round jowls and a sharp, sensitive nose which kept up a constant, interested quivering, even while the rest of it was lying quite still. Its tail was poor and rat-like; it was the part of it least like a fox, but Richard reflected that, like all young animals, it would change greatly in the months before it was fully grown. The thin tail would spray out in time into a magnificent brush, and the dull, rough coat would be transformed into a garment of gleaming fur. He put out his finger, and scratched the cub gently along its soft belly; it turned over and waved its legs, liking it.

'I thought you were going to get some mince,' said Adam, possessively.

'Yes, all right,' said Richard meekly, getting up. 'Do you think foxes eat mince?'

'We'll find that out when you bring it, won't we?' said Adam. 'He'll probably eat anything, he's so hungry. I'll fetch him some milk.'

'Well, don't use one of the good saucers,' retorted Richard, who was still nervous about the blanket. It was one of the many unfairnesses of life that he, the son of the house, was always being blasted for their combined misdemeanours, while Adam, who had established himself as a visitor, went unscathed.

He went into the stone-flagged pantry, where the deep-freezer box hummed electrically in one corner, lifted the lid, and groped painfully among the frozen packages till he found a frost-encrusted polythene bag with a hard lump of minced beef inside. He took it into the scullery, cut open the bag, and tipped the contents into a pan on the stove. The meat would have to thaw out a bit, or the little fox would break all his teeth. While he waited, warming his numb hands above the pan, Richard watched out of the corner of his eye Adam fetching a bottle of milk from the refrigerator, standing on a stool to reach down one of the best saucers in the cupboard, although there were old ones on a level with his nose, and pouring milk into it for his fox. Richard sighed, but said nothing. He would not give Adam the pleasure of knowing that he had noticed, and he knew that it was his own fault for mentioning saucers at all.

The boys watched, fascinated, while the little creature ate and drank heartily, snuffling into the half-cooked meat with his black nose, and scooping up the milk by making a cup-shape of his flexible pink tongue. Then he stretched and shook himself, turned round a couple of times on the blanket, curled himself up and shut his eyes. Richard and Adam, sitting each in an old armchair beside the fire, faced each other across the sleeping animal. They knew that a decision was going to have to be made about his future, a necessity underlined by the sound of the hall clock striking four, reminding them delicately of the passage of time.

Adam waited until the last stroke had died away into the quiet afternoon house, then he said in his rather high, clear voice, 'His name is Foxy. I'm going to keep him.'

Richard nodded assent to the first part of this remark. Foxy would do; it was a serviceable name enough. It was the second part which raised all the difficulties. He looked into Adam's pale, determined eyes and said, 'You can't keep a fox as if it was a dog.'

'Then I'll have to keep it as if it was a fox.'

Richard was patient.

'That's silly. The point is, you can't keep a fox at all.'

'You can when they're little. When he's grown up, and able to look after himself, I'll let him go.'

It was all made to sound so simple, and matter of fact, as if keeping a baby fox was something anyone could do, any day. Richard tried again.

'Adam, you'll never be allowed,' he said. 'I saw a film once, on television, about a man who tried to bring up a fox cub in his house. It was terrible. It chewed up everything in sight—pillows and books and carpets and curtains. It ripped out all the seats in a Mini, and guzzled the dashboard to ribbons, and the panelling on the doors. You never saw such a mess in your life.'

Adam glanced down at the slumbering Foxy, in admiration for his potential as a vandal. But he said coolly, 'Oh, I know I'll never be *allowed*. So I'll have to keep him secretly, won't I? Somewhere where he'll be safe from—people.'

The emphasis was slight, but Richard knew who people were. His kind, affectionate family, who had given this boy a home, and tried to treat him like a son, were people, who approved the killing of a mother fox, and could not be trusted not to murder her defenceless offspring. Still, he kept his temper. He knew from past experience that it was very difficult to have a proper fight with Adam, unless Adam started it. Otherwise, he didn't really care enough about you to fight with you; he just went away from you, and left you feeling silly and small. Besides, Adam had not yet insulted him directly.

'It's far too difficult,' Richard said. 'Don't you see—we'd have to hide him and feed him and exercise him, without anyone finding out. I don't see how we could. I think— you'd better tell Dad. He'll know what to do.'

It was what Richard would have done, in any crisis. It seemed to him the only safe and sensible thing to do, to tell his father. But to say so to Adam, in his present mood, was to invite the direct insult, and he got it. Adam's eyes blazed suddenly, and he leaned forward in his chair, clenching his red fists over his knees.

'Your Dad,' he said bitterly, now pushing firmly on to the Darkes the responsibility for atrocities. 'Your Dad shot his mother.'

Richard recoiled from the hissing acid of his voice, and he wondered how pale blue eyes could glare so hotly. But this time he was not prepared to accept the rebuke without defending himself, and his father with him.

'Listen, you,' he said dangerously, 'just you lay off my Dad. He didn't shoot that vixen for fun. If you think we can afford to lose nine hens in one night, you're an unreasonable idiot. And if you're suggesting that he'd shoot a cub—'

But Adam ignored him, and went on sarcastically as if he had not spoken.

'Fox Farm,' he said. 'Fox Farm! What a joke!' He changed to a taunting, mincing tone of voice, and went on, ' "Why do you call your place Fox Farm, Mr. Darke?" "Oh, surely you know that, sir. We shoot foxes here, to punish them for being natural." '

For a horrible, blinding moment, Richard wanted to kill him. But by the time he had spluttered out, 'It has nothing to do with foxes, you ignorant fool. It's called after a family that used to live here,' Adam had regained his usual calm indifference. He watched Richard with eyes that had gone bleak again, like a seagull's, and said flatly, 'I knew that, actually. But tell me—what would your father do with him?'

Richard was instantly deflated.

'I'm not sure,' he muttered. 'Something . . . well, I expect he would take him somewhere where it would be safe to let him go, or—or to the zoo, maybe . . .' His words tailed off into silence, as he realized he was condemning himself out of his own mouth.

'Exactly,' said Adam. 'You're not really thinking. There's nowhere safe to let him go. He couldn't look after himself, and he'd be killed, or starve to death. And,' he added fiercely, 'I'd rather either of these things happened, than have him locked up at the zoo.'

Richard shook his head. For someone who couldn't say the seven times table, and would almost certainly write the animal's name as 'Fokzy' Adam had a most clear and far-seeing mind. Richard, who was ten times as clever at school work, could never get the better of him in an argument. It was evident that they were going to hide Foxy, with all the danger and deceit which that would involve. And in the end—but there were too many problems of beginning to be faced, to start worrying yet about the end. Richard was silent for a moment, then he said rather stiffly, 'Do you want me to help you, or don't you trust me either?'

Adam knew perfectly well that his own safety depended on Richard's involvement; only then could he be sure that Richard would not give him away. But he pretended he did not care, and said with a show of unconcern, 'The point is, do you want to help me?'

'I'll help you,' Richard said. 'It'll be easier with two.'

He did not know why he said it; he owed Adam no favours. Nor was it because he felt personally responsible for the shooting, although he knew Adam wanted him to feel that he was. It had something to do with his habitual, blind loyalty to Adam, which he recognized as absurd and irrational, but really could not help.

2　*The Old Tower*

The first thing necessary, of course, was to find a hiding-place for Foxy where his barking would not attract attention, and give all three of them away. It must also be distant from those parts of the croft where Mr. Darke went every day, about his work; these considerations ruled out the stable, the old hay loft, the attic of the house, and the little outhouse at the end of the yard, which in more primitive times had been the lavatory, but was now filled with sacks and pails and garden canes. Adam wondered whether some sort of box could be erected in the rafters in the henhouse, which was a ruined cottage some distance from the farm buildings; he rather liked the idea of Mrs. Darke feeding her hens and collecting eggs with a secret fox four feet above her head. But Richard was scathing about the idea of putting even a baby fox in among hens again, and pointed out that his mother was not deaf, nor entirely stupid.

'You could trust the fox, of course, to sit in the rafters, doubled up with silent laughter,' he said sarcastically, getting his own back.

'Well, have you got a better idea?' demanded Adam.

'Yes,' said Richard. 'We'll take him down to Fox Tower.'

As soon as the old tower in the wood was mentioned, neither of the boys could imagine why they had not thought of it first of all, and saved themselves ten minutes' wondering.

'Very suitable, even to the name,' Adam said approvingly.

The clock reminded them that it was now five o'clock; darkness was already beginning to gather outside the kitchen window, and soon enough the parents would be back from their shopping trip to Millkennet, eight miles away. So

Adam went off to the loft to find an old crate and some fresh straw, while Richard somewhat guiltily helped himself to another bag of minced beef, and the remainder of the milk. He tipped the curled-up Foxy off the best blanket— mercifully unspotted—on to an old one which he had fetched from upstairs, and when everything was ready, the boys put the little animal in among the straw, and, taking turns to carry the box, hurried away from the house with their secret.

It was dark and quiet in the little wood of bent ash and beech and willow trees, planted long ago to shelter the wind-slapped fields on the river's brink, and subsequently allowed to encroach upon several acres of farmland, most of it on an adjoining property. The birds were settling to rest with only an occasional, sleepy chirp, and Adam's and Richard's feet fell noiselessly on the floor of beaten earth, carpeted with leaf mould and decaying beechmast. Richard, who had lived at Fox Farm all his life, had always felt that in the wood he was in another world; the house quickly disappeared from sight round a twist in the track, and the walls of unthinned trees seemed to shut out all the familiar sounds of the farmyard and the plain beyond, dogs barking, the stream chuckling, machinery whirring, the quick, hoarse cry of sea-gulls sailing on the breast of the wind. In summer, there was a soft inner sighing of leaves, but now, in winter, the sky was of net, or like looking through the holes in loose knitting. It was so silent as to be a little unnerving; Richard, who imagined things, was glad to have the fearless Adam stamping along at his side, carrying the crate with Foxy in his wiry arms. Richard could hear the comfortable, spluttering little snores of the creature, as he burrowed cosily under the blanket, and he experienced a rush of deep thankfulness that Adam had found Foxy in time. It would have been so dreadful if he had had to spend the night out of doors, and died of exposure, and they had found his little body on the croft next day. Richard still did not know what chance Foxy had of growing up, and living the life for which he was intended by nature, but he was glad that he and Adam were going to give him as good a chance as they could—whatever the consequences.

The tower rose abruptly out of the trees, a huge stone pepper-pot with a mouldy wooden door, some narrow, un-glazed windows, and broken crenellations around its flat roof. It seemed misplaced and forlorn, pushing up its aged head above the pale grass and branches which pressed on it, writhing through its window spaces and trying to choke its door, an unlovely ruin standing useless between the quiet croft and the polluted waters of the widening estuary. Its day was long past; hundreds of years ago it had been built as a watch-tower, to guard the river crossing; later, a dwelling house had been built adjoining it, but both had been abandoned when peace came between the Highlands and Lowlands in the eighteenth century, and the inhabitants grew weary of living in a building which filled with water every time there was a spell of heavy rain. The house had fallen into disrepair, and had been demolished so long ago that the Darkes did not even know of its existence, but the tower with its seven-foot walls defied the destroyers, and stood grimly on long after it had ceased to serve any important purpose. Successive tenants of the croft had kept pigs in it, stored their implements in it, allowed the Scouts and Guides to camp in it. Mr. Darke, some years ago, had decided that the upper storeys were becoming unsafe, and had sealed off the foot of the stair with a rough brick wall. David kept his rowing boat in the downstairs room; Richard rarely went near the place at all.

Because Adam's arms were full of Foxy, Richard turned the clammy handle, and pushed against the dank, swollen door. It gave way reluctantly, and a coldly stuffy smell wafted out of the enclosed interior. Leaving the door open, the boys edged down the narrow stone passage into the round chamber, with its low ceiling and unplastered walls covered with a greening of thin moss. The tower was almost on the river bank, and the tide came seeping into its foundation. The rowing boat, raised on trestles and draped in a tarpaulin, loomed in the centre of the floor, slightly alarming in the gloom, like a stiff-legged beast. Very little light filtered through the three slit-windows.

'Does David come down here often?' asked Adam, eyeing the boat suspiciously.

'Not at this time of year,' replied Richard, noticing how flat and hollow even Adam's voice sounded in this place. 'He's only allowed to take the boat out in summer, and in any case, he's far too busy swotting for O-levels just now to have time for anything else.'

'That's all right, then,' said Adam, casting his eye around for the best place to put Foxy's box. 'Over there, I think,' he went on, as if answering himself, 'where there's a little alcove in the wall. He'll be out of the draught from the door, and we'll put his food beside him on the floor.'

'Yes,' Richard agreed. But he glanced round the desolate room again, and added, uncertainly, 'Only—Adam, this is not a very nice place, is it? I mean, I wouldn't like to spend the night here.'

Now that his eyes had become accustomed to the poor light, he could see Adam's pale face grinning at him. But he did not feel offended, because it was not one of Adam's jeering grins. Almost friendly, in fact.

'You're not a fox,' Adam pointed out, as he went to

deposit Foxy's bed against the wall, pushing it firmly into the alcove where once a fireplace had been. 'I don't suppose they're so pernickety about where they lie down. This is probably a palace, compared with where he's been other nights. Now give me the mince and the milk, and stop being so daft.'

His tone was strong and confident; he was in a good temper, exulting because he was getting things all his own way. Well, let him exult, thought Richard rather grimly, as they closed the tower door and sped back through the chilly wood to the house. Foxy had a warm bed for the night, and food for the morning, but if Adam thought that Mrs. Darke tossed bags of meat into the deep-freezer without counting them, or that milk flowed from the refrigerator in a never-ending stream, he was the one who was daft. Somehow, he would have to be made to realize that the real problems were only beginning.

Richard's parents had had their monthly treat of tea out at the hotel in Millkennet, but Mrs. Darke had fried eggs and sausages for the boys on her return. After they had washed up, Richard and Adam went into the sitting-room to watch a film on television. They were both distracted by private thoughts of Foxy, lying alone in his box in the dark tower room, but they did not have an opportunity to talk again until much later, when they were in bed. Then Richard, whose weekly turn it was for the bottom bunk, switched off the light, and said firmly into the darkness, 'There are things we'll have to discuss.'

'Such as?'

'Well, feeding him, for one,' said Richard, arranging his hot-water bottle between his knees and pulling his covers up to his chin. 'Foxy is going to eat a lot of food, and we'll have to decide where it's to come from.'

The silence which followed confirmed his suspicion that Adam had thought the deep-freezer an open invitation to theft in a good cause.

He pressed on, 'We can't go on helping ourselves to meat twice a day, surely you see that. Mother would notice in no time, and we'd never be able to dream up a convincing excuse for pinching *mince*, for heaven's sake. And she only buys four pints of milk a day—enough for us, but there won't be any to spare for Foxy. And besides—' he expected Adam to be sneery about this, but it had to be said '—I'm not going to steal from my own parents, and I don't see why you should either.' He was going to say, 'They feed you. Why should they feed your fox as well?' but decided in time that it sounded churlish, so he said instead, 'They don't have a lot of money—Dad says times are very bad. So if we've decided to keep Foxy, it's up to us to feed him.'

But Adam, who was touchy beyond what was normal, had extracted Richard's meaning from what he had not said, and before asking, 'How do you suggest we feed him, then?' he could not resist remarking stiffly, 'Your parents don't keep me for nothing, you know. They get money every week from the Social Work Department. I don't owe you anything.'

Richard, who did not want to be side-tracked into an unpleasant and fruitless argument, ignored the remark, and answered the question.

'We can buy his food.'

'What with?'

'Our pocket money.'

'Not enough,' said Adam quickly; relievedly, Richard thought.

'Then we must use our savings,' he insisted. 'You never spend anything, so you must have lots put away.'

Adam, who never spent anything because he read Richard's comics, ate his sweets, gave paltry and grudging presents, and never went anywhere if he had to pay, did not like this suggestion at all. He had ten pounds in fifty-pence pieces squirrelled away in a sugar bag in the suitcase under the bed, the fruits of much miserly hoarding of pocket money. But that was his going-to-Australia money: it was not to be squandered on meat for a fox. Only—of course. There was the loop-hole he needed. *It was a fox.*

So he said suddenly, 'What do foxes eat in the wild?'

'Hens,' replied Richard bitterly.

'Oh, yes, I know. Poor old hens,' said Adam callously. 'But they don't eat them for every meal, I suppose. What do they eat when they can't get hens?'

'I don't know.'

'You're supposed to know. You've seen a film about one. What did it eat, when it wasn't guzzling carpets?'

'It was a long time ago,' said Richard defensively. It was true that he could remember nothing about the film except the shots of the restless little animal chewing up books and a quilt, and the shredded upholstery in the patient film-maker's car. 'But we could look up a book,' he suggested.

'Do you have one?'

'No, but David has. Animals were one of his crazes, before geology, I think. One Christmas Dad gave him a marvellous book, all about wildlife—a waste of money, if you think what David's like. I know where it is. We'll have to be careful with it, though—he's terribly fussy about his things.'

Rather unwillingly, for he was by now very comfortable, Richard got up, and went next door to David's room, switching on the light as he went in. The place was cold, and extremely tidy, most unlike the room that Richard shared with Adam. The older boy's books were set out carefully on his home-made bookshelves, his fossils and geology specimens displayed in the beautiful baize-lined box, with a glass top, which he had made in the woodwork class at Millkennet High School. Even his posters looked as if they had been checked with a spirit-level before being tacked on to the walls. Richard felt guilty amid such order; he tiptoed furtively over to the bookshelves, and found the volume he wanted on the bottom shelf, among David's other nature books. It was called *A Concise Guide to the Wildlife of the British Isles*, but it was not very concise; it was heavy with pages and information. Richard carried it back to his own room, where Adam had put on the light, and was sitting up in bed, rubbing the brightness out of his screwed-up eyes. Richard got back under the covers and set the book across his knees, thankfully pressing his cold soles to the hot-water bottle, and began to look up the index, under 'F'.

' "FOX, COMMON",' he announced. 'That'll be it. Page two hundred and fourteen.'

Adam swung down suddenly, and hung upside-down like a bat over the edge of the upper bunk. Richard could not help laughing at him, with his eyes where his mouth should be, and his nostrils pointing in the wrong direction.

'You look funny,' he said.

'Come on, come on,' said Adam impatiently. 'I can't hang around here all night.'

Richard laughed again; he thought Adam was very witty. He found page two hundred and fourteen, where there was a column of print alongside a magnificent photograph of a fully grown fox, resplendent in russet fur, with a sharp, clever little face pushing out from a background of tawny bracken. Adam squinted at the photograph, while Richard read aloud, ' "Common Fox. *Vulpes vulpes*—" '

'Eh?' interrupted Adam.

'It's Latin,' explained Richard patiently, 'for a common fox.'

'Pooh, stupid,' said Adam.

'"*Vulpes vulpes,*"' repeated Richard emphatically, and read on. '"The fur of this animal is thick, and may be variable in colour. Its legs are long and slender, although in its thick winter coat it may look short in the leg. The common fox inhabits woods, undergrowth and reed thickets, but is seldom seen, for he is shy and wary, and often hunts at night. When looking for food, the fox keeps its snout close to the ground, but at other times carries its head erect, and its tail downward. Foxes do much harm by eating poultry and hares, but do much good by eating mice, which they can dig from underground. They also eat grasshoppers, dung beetles and insects, and in autumn berries, and other fruits within reach. Sometimes they bury stores as reserves before the birth of cubs, or against winter shortages. The lair or earth usually has several access tunnels; the young are born in early spring, March–April. The vixen carries back food to the young, and by June they are able to wander about in search of insects, or on mouse hunts."'

There was silence for a few moments, while they considered all this information. Adam's upside-down face, which had been turning purple, disappeared, to reappear almost immediately.

'What's a dung beetle?' he asked.

'Well, use your head,' said Richard. 'We're certainly not going looking for them. Insects are out altogether, at this time of year, and berries too. We could probably catch him some mice, though,' he said, brightening. 'This house is full of them—you can hear them scampering about in the attic, and down the sides of the walls. There are traps in the cupboard. Or maybe he could catch his own, down in the tower. But not till June,' he added regretfully, glancing down at the book again.

'If they don't eat him first,' said Adam, a ghoulish look coming over his inverted face. 'I heard a story once about a kitten—'

'I don't want to hear it,' said Richard violently.

Really, Adam was dreadful. He was the one determined to keep the fox, who had been so anxious to make up a cosy bed for him, where he would be out of the draught, and have food for the night. Yet he could relish horrible stories about young animals being eaten by mice. It wasn't natural.

Adam lay down, grinning, and squirmed down under the bedclothes. He was laughing softly to himself. He had never heard a story about a kitten, but he would happily have made one up on the spur of the moment, just for the fun of seeing Richard's face.

Mrs. Darke came upstairs, and scolded them for having the light on when it was nearly eleven o'clock. Yet she did it mildly; she had been aware, at tea time, of the tingling in the air which indicated, even without nods and signs and catching of the eye, that the boys were sharing a secret. She was pleased, and astonished that, after two years of separateness, Richard and Adam should have a secret, but it did not even occur to her to wonder what it was. She was fat and kind, and she would have been happy had she not been worrying all the time because her hens did not lay, and her cabbages were going for a song at Millkennet market, but, like Adam, she had no imagination whatsoever.

When she had closed the door, and gone away to bed, Richard said decisively into the darkness, 'That's settled, then. We set mousetraps, and buy the rest of his food with our own money.'

The upper mattress creaked as Adam writhed in protest. 'I suppose,' he conceded unenthusiastically.

He could see that it must be so, if Richard was determined to be unhelpful about the deep-freezer, but he very much hoped that Foxy would quickly develop a taste for mice.

3 *The Foster-Child*

If the Darkes thought that Adam Hewitt disliked them, they were mistaken. Indeed, he liked them better than any people he had ever known, except his father, and if he had been fair, he would have had to admit that they had been kinder to him than his father had ever been. But it had nothing to do with kindness; still, after six years of separation, Adam wanted to be with his father, with an ache of wanting that nothing and no one else could ever satisfy. And he would be with him one day, perhaps soon; any time now, a letter might come from his father in Australia, inviting him to come and join him on the sheep farm in New South Wales where he had gone to work. And when that happened, Adam did not want his joy spoiled by regret for the people he was leaving. So he kept himself aloof from the Darkes, as he had kept himself aloof from all the other people he had lived among, sorry for their puzzlement and disappointment, but not sorry enough to do anything to make them feel better. He had cherished his separateness so long that it was becoming his reality.

Years ago, when he had been a little boy, Adam had lived in a flat in a Glasgow street, with a father and mother, like anyone else. He could just remember his mother, a red-headed woman in a blue dress; when he thought about her, Adam always saw her in the same blue dress. They had been happy, he and his father and mother; they had gone shopping, and sometimes to the zoo on Saturdays, and once they had spent a week by the sea. Adam could remember paddling in glinting summer water, reaching up to hold on to his father's finger. His head had been on a level with his father's bare thigh, and whenever he evoked that day, he could see again, in close-up, the short, strong gold hairs growing on the man's sunburnt skin, the drops of salt water clinging to them like beads in the sunshine. It gave him a vivid sense of his father, to remember that.

But his mother had died, giving birth to his little sister, and a few days later, the baby had died too. These things didn't happen often nowadays, he had heard people say, but they did happen, and they had happened to him, and to his family. Things had changed for the worse after that; his father had begun to stay out late, and come home flushed and smelling of whisky, and when the neighbours had threatened to report him to the police for leaving a child alone in the house at night, a child-minder had appeared. Her name was Ruby, and she used to slap Adam when they were alone, and pet him and try to kiss him in front of his father. Adam had hated her, and begged his father to send her away, but his father had only got angry, and shouted, and told him to mind his manners, and chased him out into the street to play. It had come as no surprise to Adam when they got married, Andrew Hewitt and Ruby Frazer; Adam was sent away to spend the week-end with his aunt at Dumbarton.

He had stayed with his father and Ruby for a few months after that, but there was never any hope of reconciliation; she knew that he had tried to get rid of her, and she hated him as much as he hated her. And when Adam's father had decided to emigrate, and start a new life in far-off Australia, Ruby had seen her chance, and had told him that he must choose between her and Adam.

'You have to make up your mind which of us you prefer, Hew, for you can't have both. If that brat goes, I stay.'

The brat stayed, she went.

After that, Adam had gone back briefly to stay with his mother's sister and her husband at Dumbarton, but they had a small house, and children of their own, and they didn't really want him either. Real trouble had arisen when money stopped coming from Australia to pay for Adam's food and clothing; in less than a year he found himself in the care of the city Social Work Department, living sometimes in a Children's Home, sometimes with families who tried to be kind, but soon grew tired of the remote, watchful child who never showed a spark of affection for anyone. They could not possibly have understood that for Adam, it was as if none of this was really happening, that he regarded it as a temporary interruption of the real continuity of his life. Never for a moment did Adam doubt that the breakdown of his relationship with his father was for a little time only, an unfortunate accident, a situation which would be magically reversed, today, tomorrow, or the next day. For he loved his father, and he was convinced that his father really loved him. It was all Ruby's fault; she was the wicked witch who had put a spell on his father. But the spell would be broken. One day soon, the man would realize that a son is more important than a second-choice wife; he would send Ruby away, and send for Adam to come and join him. It was in his mind now, Adam was sure, for once—only three years ago—he had sent his son a postcard from Australia. It was captioned, *Sunset over Katoomba*, and showed a great expanse of violent, copper-red sky, reflecting fire on to wooded, cliff-hung mountains of incredible ruggedness, beyond which stretched an indeterminate purple landscape, with darker mountains still on the horizon. It gave Adam an awesome feeling of the vastness of the earth; he longed to escape out of this small, mean cage of industrial Scotland, and fly away across the world to the wide-open land of

Australia. And it was his father's wish too, of that he was certain, for on the back he had written, 'Have been to the mountains on a camping holiday. You would like it here. So long. Dad.'

No more postcards had ever come, but it was enough. 'You would like it here. So long. Dad.' That was the short, postcard way of saying, 'I'm missing you, and I want you to be here with me. I'll see you soon. . . .'

Adam had kept the postcard in his suitcase, along with his mother's watch, which he had been allowed to keep because Ruby already had a better one, and a tattered travel brochure advertising *Australia, Land of Opportunity*. And he began to save, every penny that came his way, in the sugar bag which he had picked up in the kitchen of the Children's Home. It would never do to arrive without money in the Land of Opportunity.

And so, still waiting for his summons to a new life, Adam had come to the Darkes, and for the first time he had had to fight against the temptation to put down a little root, and respond to kindness with love. It was the first time he had ever been fostered in a country place, and he liked the little croft, the dark, damp old house of ancient stone and pantile, the restless, changing river on one side and the wide plain on the other, warm and fruitful in summer with wheat and barley and green pasture, in winter a patchwork of sleeping fields, grey and fawn and lime, bordered by black hawthorn hedges, like strips of broken lace. He liked the wind that blew from the north, bending the poplars as easily as blades of grass, and the great, shifting arc of the sky.

And he liked the people; the crofter father, in his blue dungarees and old brown jersey, a quiet man with huge, earth-worn hands and dark eyes alert to every change in the weather, the large, cheerful mother who had not insulted him with Dettol baths and a complete new wardrobe. He liked Richard, too, acknowledging his tolerance even while he goaded him to relieve his own half-admitted feelings of jealousy and loneliness; the older children, Anne, who was away from home a lot, and David, did not affect his life very much, though they were always nice to him. But Adam withstood the temptation to love any of them; his resolve held. They must not come between him and his dream of Australia, and his father.

And now there was Foxy.

Long after Richard had fallen asleep, Adam lay awake, more intensely awake than ever in the middle of the day, shaking the bunk beds with his turning and tossing to and fro. Last night, in spite of his pity for the fox, it had been almost a relief to have a grudge to hold against the Darkes, because that made it so much easier to resist affection. They had willed the death of a free, wild thing, and today, when he had found the little animal beside the road, his feeling had erupted into a passion of righteous anger against those who had killed a mother and left a baby to fend for itself. He had thought of nothing except that he wanted to keep it and give it a chance to grow up to freedom and a good life. For, although he had never put the idea into words, he believed that everyone had a right to these things, both people and animals. The difference was that people could think, and plot for the things they wanted; animals could not. That was why he had bullied Richard, involving him in the affair so that he could not possibly tell his parents.

His triumph over Richard had carried Adam pleasantly through the evening; he could not look at him without feeling a pleased smirk twitching the corners of his mouth. Only now, as he lay in the deep night, thinking of Foxy sleeping down at the tower in his bed of straw, did the mass of problems which always seem ten times as bad in the dark as in the day, come bubbling to the surface of his mind. He wondered if he had been unwise.

It was the matter of the money, of course, which hit him hardest. He had assumed, if he had thought at all, that there would be no problem about feeding Foxy; Richard, once involved in theft, would continue discreetly to remove bags of meat from the freezer, and a saucer of milk for Foxy should be as easy to obtain as a glass of milk for oneself. Adam had not reckoned on Richard's stubbornness, and he had been angry with him for refusing to go on stealing, but try as he might to be at the same time detached and thoroughly unfair, he could not help seeing the other boy's point of view. Mrs. Darke was Richard's mother, and you did not steal from your mother—especially if she had counted the things you were planning to steal. Moreover, the Darkes were worried about money at the moment; they could not get decent prices for their pigs at the market, it had been a disastrous year for potatoes, and most of the cabbages had been eaten to fine lace by voracious caterpillars. Mr. Darke had even mentioned looking for another job, at which the whole family had turned white and silent. The financial worries of parents always had a bad effect on children; Adam had observed this at his aunt's at Dumbarton, and in other places where he had lived. And he could appreciate Richard's argument that stealing over a long period was not a good idea; once she had found them out, Mrs. Darke would not rest till she had discovered how the meat had been disposed of. She was that kind of woman. Very thorough.

Nonetheless, the idea of having to contribute to Foxy's well-being out of his own pocket did not please Adam in the very least. Every Saturday, at lunch time, Mr. Darke gave out the pocket money, a pound note to David and twenty-five pence each to Adam and Richard. Adam immediately carried his upstairs, and put it away safely in the sugar bag; about once a month, he asked Mrs. Darke to change the ten and five-pence coins for fifty-pence pieces, which he liked better than pound notes, because they were more substantial. Sometimes, if Richard was occupied elsewhere, he would sit down on the bottom bunk and tip the pile of heavy, satisfying coins on to the quilt. He would pick them up in twos, and make little piles, counting the pounds carefully, as if he did not already know down to the last penny how much was there. He never seemed to get much beyond ten pounds. Christmas kept coming, and the Darkes would keep having birthdays, and Mrs. Darke didn't like it if he ignored these occasions completely. Now, in March, he had thought there would be no more calls on his sugar bag till October. Instead of which, he realized angrily, the ten pounds he had now would soon be converted into food for a fox. He would arrive penniless in the Land of Opportunity. For a moment, Adam wished passionately that he had ignored the little cries in the grass, that he had done what he usually did, had the sense to look after himself and let the rest of the world take its chance. Yet when he remembered the bright little face with its liquid honey eyes, tender ears and eager, thrusting nose, and experienced again the thrill of delight he had felt when he opened his jerkin and Foxy had jumped right in, next to his chest, as if he belonged there, Adam knew that he did not really wish it so. It was a pity about the money, but Foxy was worth it; already, in some obscure way, he knew that he would be wrong to press for his own chance of life, while denying Foxy his.

4 *Sunday*

Day on the croft began early or lasted till late; in winter, everyone in the house was up before daylight, and in summer they were often still working in the field or garden after nine o'clock at night. The boys' morning chores consisted of feeding the hens and looking for eggs, and carrying pails of food to the gluttonous tenants of the pigsty; twice a week, on market days, they also had to help pack the van, which left for Millkennet at eight o'clock. Usually these tasks had to be accomplished before school, but the coming of the week-end made no difference to getting up time, because pigs got hungry at the same hour on Saturday and Sunday as they did on other days of the week. Every two weeks, however, one of the boys had a Sunday off, and now it was Richard's turn, so Adam was surprised when he slid down from his bunk at half-past six next morning, in answer to Mrs. Darke's insistent drum-beat on the wall, and found Richard already up, pulling on his trousers.

'It's your day off,' groaned Adam, who was stiff and sandy-eyed from lack of sleep. 'Had you forgotten?'

'No,' said Richard. 'I thought I'd come and give you a hand. If I do the pigs while you do the hens, we can be finished in half the time, then we can run down to the tower and see Foxy before breakfast.'

Adam knew that it was a decent thing to do, and more than he would have done for Richard. He would have stayed warmly in bed, until the clanking of pails outside the window told him that Richard had finished at the henhouse and gone off to the sty, then he would have got out of bed, dressed quickly, and slipped down to the tower alone, before Richard came back. Only, of course, he would have had a perfect right to do so, he reminded himself hastily. For Foxy belonged to him. Still—'Well, thanks,' he said gruffly. 'You needn't have.'

The morning was pearl grey and cold, with mist lying over the wood like thin smoke. The boys parted on the doorstep with a whispered, 'Don't be long,' Adam making off in the direction of the henhouse, with his basket of meal, while Richard plodded down the yard to the sty, balanced by two pails of steaming swill. His breath blew out in front of him, vapour that vanished and was constantly renewed in the cold air. Usually he liked feeding the stout, sandy pigs, who had so much more personality than hens; there were four at the moment, Polly and Molly, Wilkins and Charles the Fat. They lumbered to their feet as he pushed open the door of the sty, and pressed eagerly forward out of the straw, their pink, snouty faces jovial and quite unembarrassed by the terrible scent they wore. Richard enjoyed filling the zinc troughs with food, and watching them jostling for a good position, pushing each other out of the way with their incredible behinds. But today, his mind was on other things; as he watered the animals and swept the concrete floor of the sty, he was desperately anxious to know how little Foxy had passed the night. He was so afraid that they would find him scratching at the inside of the tower door, whining to get out. He knew from the anxious look in Adam's eyes, as he came flying back down the path from the henhouse, that he had had the same thought; it was a relief to drop pails and baskets, and run down through the wood to the tower.

The sun was up now, but veiled by a thick bank of low cloud. The birds were up too, filling the air with clear morning music for anyone who had time to listen. The boys had not: they made straight for the tower, straining their ears beyond the birdsong for distant barking. But there was none. They reached the door, and pushed ahead into the stillness of the stone room. Now they were panting, and as afraid as if they had been greeted with cries of distress.

A first glance round the gloomy place suggested that nothing had been moved, and they looked at each other with wild eyes that said, 'He escaped,' or, 'He died in the night.' It was Richard who first had courage to walk over to the box; he knelt down, and twitched the ruffled blanket aside. A warmth emanated from the straw, comforting him. Foxy was lying curled up in a ball, breathing steadily. He opened one yellow eye, and winked at Richard.

'Adam, he's all right,' Richard said softly. 'Come and see.'

C871990 co. schools

Adam came, and knelt down beside him on the damp stone. Richard could feel the waves of the other boy's relief, wilder and stronger than his own.

'Lazy little beggar,' said Adam to Foxy, putting out his hand to rub the animal behind its ears. Richard was startled by the unaccustomed gentleness in Adam's voice. Foxy squirmed ecstatically, uncurling his thin tail for Adam, and waving it in the air.

'He knows me,' said Adam, incredulous and proud.

Richard left them together, and began to examine the room. He could see, from the location of some droppings and little pools of water, that Foxy had explored it fairly thoroughly; he was also relieved to see that he had eaten the mince, and drunk most, but not all of his milk, then had the sense to go back to bed. Richard tried to point these things out to Adam, but Adam was sitting on the floor now, allowing Foxy to explore him; Foxy was in Adam's pocket, down the open neck of his shirt; he was licking Adam's face, pushing his nose up Adam's trouser leg, all the time tick-tocking with his ridiculous tail, and uttering little puppy yaps of delight. Adam was radiant; he said, 'Yes, yes,' to everything Richard said, but Richard knew it was all going in one ear and out of the other. He watched the boy with shy curiosity; it was like seeing a flower open.

Richard added milk to Foxy's saucer from the bottle which they had left behind the previous day, then he said, 'Adam, we'll have to go. It's breakfast time.' He had to say it three times before Adam got up reluctantly, and put Foxy back in his box. The little creature peeped brightly at him over the wooden edge of the box, ears pricked, not understanding.

'We'll be back soon, Foxy,' promised Richard. 'Oh, *come on*, Adam!' he added, seeing Adam kneel down to start the game all over again.

'You'll have to realize,' went on Richard severely, as they hurried back over the soft carpet of the wood, 'that we mustn't start being late for meals, because of Foxy. Mother doesn't like it, and it's the first thing that will make her start asking questions. And once she starts asking questions, she doesn't stop till she gets answers.'

It was just what Adam had thought last night, when pondering the pros and cons of stealing mince. But he did not want to think about it now. He was still revelling in the memory of the warm, confiding brown body nestling close to his chest, and the rough, eager tongue against his neck. And he hated leaving Foxy alone in that place; this was the foretaste of many grievous partings.

Richard made Adam clean the earth and leaves and tiny twigs off his boots before they went into the house; he could see that he was the one who would have to attend to practical details. At breakfast, Adam ate with absorption, and said nothing, but this was usual.

The rest of the morning was occupied with homework, and Church, which was frustrating, but inevitable. Not till after lunch, when Mr. and Mrs. Darke had departed thankfully into the sitting-room, for their Sunday afternoon sleep behind the newspapers, were the boys free to change into old clothes, and go down to the tower again, this time laden with logs, and Mr. Darke's tool bag, and a cardboard carton full of odds and ends which Richard thought would contribute to Foxy's comfort and safety.

'There's this collar and lead that used to belong to our old dog Shep,' he said. 'It'll be useful for teaching Foxy to walk at heel. We don't want him running away and getting lost in the wood. And I've found Shep's drinking bowl—it won't tip over as easily as a saucer. And I suppose—' he frowned uneasily '—I'd better grab another bag of mince, to see him over until we get to the shops tomorrow.'

Adam nodded, feeling rebuked, although there was no reproach in Richard's tone. Foxy was his, after all, yet it was Richard who thought of all these arrangements for his well-being.

Always, afterwards, Adam would remember that Sunday afternoon as one of the happiest times of his life. It was a flat, grey winter afternoon, with no beauty of nature or fine weather to make it memorable, but he was happy because he was doing what, at that moment, he most wanted to do. For once, he forgot the future, and Australia, and keeping himself private and uninvolved, and simply concentrated on enjoying now.

This time, Foxy was out of his box when they arrived, nosing inquisitively around the trestles which supported the boat; he turned as they came through the narrow opening into the room, and hurtled across the floor to greet them, yelping and waving in a frenzy of welcome. The boys dropped their burdens, and squatted down to make a fuss of him; Foxy rubbed round Richard's legs, and pushed his nose into Richard's hand, as if unwilling to hurt his feelings by leaving him out, but it was under Adam's hands that he writhed elastically with pleasure, rolling over and trying to catch the boy's fingers in his mouth, and when the two got up, it was Adam he went after, getting in between his ankles and trying to climb on to the toes of his shoes.

'Let's take him out first,' Richard suggested. 'We'll have to find time to give him a run every day—you can't keep an animal cooped up in a place like this without exercise and fresh air. And we'll have to try to train him,' he added, looking disapprovingly at the trail of puddles all over the floor. He had a good farmer's dislike of a dirty steading.

Privately, Adam doubted that you could train a fox to be fussy about such matters, but he did not waste time saying so to Richard; he was longing to be out in the wood with Foxy.

They had some difficulty in persuading the little beast to wear Shep's old collar; he definitely did not like the idea, and said so, resisting indignantly while the boys tried to hold his leaping body still, and buckle the leather strap round his thin neck. Eventually Adam had to straddle him, holding his front paws in his hands and his haunches between his knees, while Richard slipped the collar over the rotating head. Then they fastened on the lead, and were off at the gallop. Foxy set the pace, and it was a furious one; once out of the tower, he dashed here and there, intoxicated with strange scents, rushing at a pecking starling in a clearing, trying to get down rabbit holes, dragging Adam through the bramble thickets so that he was yelling with the pain of his scratches at the same time as he was helpless with laughter. Foxy was in five places at once, getting his spindle-shanks tangled in the lead, so that every so often his feet went out beneath him, and he landed on his furry chin in the bracken. Richard rushed after them, in and out of the trees, uttering hoots of merriment; he thought he had never seen anything so funny in his life.

Eventually, Foxy tired, and calmed down, so that the return to the tower was more sedate; he seemed to be getting the idea of walking on the lead, and trotted between his friends, looking pleased with himself, and them.

Back in the tower, he lay down between the boys on his blanket, while they set about the jobs which Richard said needed to be done. The main task was to improve the bed, and Richard had a clear picture in his mind's eye of what he wanted to do. First of all, he turned all the straw out of the box, and, with a small saw from his father's tool bag, cut a half-moon shape from one side, so that Foxy would still be able to get into it when it was raised from the damp floor. Then he set a log under each corner, like a stout leg, and drove long nails into it through the bottom of the box. It was a rough job, but effective; when the bedding had been replaced, and the box put back in its sheltered alcove, Foxy obligingly got up, leaped into it, and out again, with the air of one giving a demonstration. Then he lay down across Adam's knees, and fell asleep.

Adam was adorning Shep's old drinking bowl with blue paint; he had found a tin and some brushes which David had used last summer to touch up the rowing boat. He painted some hens, with legs like Wellington boots, then he said, 'How do you spell "Foxy"?'

'F, O, X, Y,' said Richard. 'Honestly, Adam, you should learn your spelling at night.'

'I could, if I liked, but what do I need spelling for?' said Adam indifferently. All school work seemed a waste of time

to him, unnecessary lumber for a person destined to spend
his life raising sheep in New South Wales. Therefore, he
did not waste his energy on it, whatever Mrs. Darke and his
teachers had to say on the subject. He had been to nine
schools since he was five, and he had heard it all before:
'Could do better. Intelligent but lazy. Shows little interest.'

He dipped his brush, and painted a curly 'F' on the side
of the dish that had no hens. Richard grinned at him, and he
grinned back, and it was as if they were friends, there in that
strange little room.

Richard had found David's duckboard leaning against the
wall, and as Adam went on painting, he lay down on it,
looking up at the vaulted roof of the tower room, which was
a continuation of the stone walls, but gathered to a peak at
the centre. It was rather beautiful, despite the damp, and
not at all rough, like the outside of the building; ribs of
chiselled pink stone, in contrast with the grey, ran in curved
lines from floor to apex, centring on a carved coat-of-arms,
which now caught Richard's attention for the first time.

'Look,' he said to Adam, pointing upwards. 'It's the same
coat-of-arms as the one you see on the Fauxe family
memorial in Garlet Church—a fox standing up on its hind
legs, a tower and a cup. My teacher says the tower is this
one, and the cup is the one in the story of the Weird.'

'The what?' said Adam, glancing up at the ceiling. He
was not interested in coats-of-arms, but the strange word
caught his attention.

'The Weird. It means a curse.'

'What curse?'

'The curse on the House of Fauxe. It's a legend, about
the family that used to stay down here, but now they live up
at Garlet Place, you know. Apparently away back in the
sixteenth century, some old ancestor of theirs stole a

Communion cup from Garlet Church, and the priest put a curse on the family, by bell, book and candle, so it was sure to come true. He said that if the cup was not returned to the Church by a Fauxe, the family would lose its titles and half its lands, and would die out altogether in the thirteenth generation. And before you begin to mock—' he wagged a warning finger '—you should know that it seems to have come true. In Jacobite times, the Fauxes came out for the Pretender, and George II took away their title and more than half their land as a punishment. They were Lord Fauxes before that.'

'Pure coincidence,' said Adam cynically.

'Well, yes. That's what everybody thought. But now there's this very queer business about Mrs. Fauxe's son.'

Mrs. Fauxe was Mr. Darke's landlord, and Adam knew her by sight, a tall, tweedy old lady with bright eyes and a hawk-nose, and thin old legs of the kind that ought to have bird's feet at the ends of them instead of brogues.

'What about her son?' he asked, interested in spite of himself.

'He's disappeared, that's what about him,' replied Richard. 'He is—was—a Major in the Scots Guards. About a year ago, he was on an Army expedition to the Amazon, and one day he went out with a party to reconnoitre, and never came back. He hasn't been heard of since.'

'And he was the thirteenth generation.'

'Yes. Mrs. Fauxe told Mother she'd never believed in the Weird, and she didn't even know Robert *was* the thirteenth generation till she counted up.'

'Does she believe he's dead?'

'She says not, but after all these months, I suppose she must wonder, poor woman.'

Adam stuck his paintbrush back in the pot, pushed Foxy

gently off his legs, and got up, shaking off the influence of Richard's story, and Mrs. Fauxe's distress, like a dog shaking water off its coat.

'Oh, well, we've all got troubles,' he said carelessly.

Richard felt a little spurt of anger, and wanted to say quickly, 'Only we don't all concentrate on our own the way you do.' But he did not intend to spoil a happy afternoon with a useless last-minute quarrel, so instead he began to put the tools back in the tool bag, and said, 'It's nearly five o'clock—we'll really have to be going now.'

This time, leaving was much worse than it had been in the morning. The boys set out Foxy's food for the night, and put him down under the blanket in his box, hoping to be able to slip away while he was not looking. But he sensed that he was being abandoned; with ears alert and wide, beseeching eyes, he ran in front of them, trying to head them off, crying to come too. When they did succeed in getting past him, and closing the door, they could hear him scratching and whining pathetically inside.

'He'll go back when we're gone. He'll be all right,' Richard tried to say reassuringly, but he found he was speaking to the air. Adam had run off, helter-skelter up the path, desperate to put silence between himself and the sad little reproaches of betrayal.

After tea, when Richard's parents and David, who had come home during the afternoon, had gone back into the sitting-room, Richard and Adam fetched out the mousetraps from the cupboard in the scullery. There were eight of them, and a rat trap, which they discarded.

'I don't think we have any rats, and it could cut off our fingers, if it went off accidentally,' said Richard, shuddering at the strength of the wicked steel spring.

'Cheese,' said Adam. 'We need cheese.'

They cut off a thick slice from the wedge of Cheddar in the refrigerator, and went up to the attic at the top of the house, a great, dark, musty tent of a place, noisy with rattling tiles and windy voices. Richard had always been afraid of it, and nothing in the world would have persuaded him to go up alone, even in daylight, for it was full of thick shadows and the creaking of the house's ancient bones. But with Adam, nothing was frightening in quite the same way. Richard had only to think that a few old chairs, stacked in a corner with their legs bristling in all directions, looked like a giant insect in the gloom, and panic seized his throat, but as soon as Adam, spotting the resemblance but unabashed by it, had pulled a ghastly face and cried, 'Eek, ooh, a-ahrgh, it's coming to get us,' he laughed, and the insect was a pile of old chairs again. Adam held a torch, while Richard broke up the cheese, and set the traps, placing them at intervals between the heavy joists.

'Do you suppose Foxy will like mice?' asked Richard doubtfully.

'He'd better,' said Adam, thinking of the imminent reduction in his savings. He found it easier to be severe with Foxy when he was away from him.

There was silence for a while, as they crawled about in the dust and crumbling plaster, then Richard said tentatively, 'Adam, I've been wondering.'

'Tell me your wonders, my little man.'

'What happened to the rest of the cubs.'

Shocked out of his witty mood, Adam raised his torch involuntarily, and shone it full in Richard's face, like a searchlight. 'Eh?' he said.

Richard threw himself aside out of the painful circle of light. Then he could see Adam's face, shadowy behind the torch, but looking blank, uncomprehending.

'What cubs, for heaven's sake?'

Richard laid down the last trap, and sat across one joist, with his feet on another.

'The rest of the litter,' he said. 'A vixen wouldn't only have one cub. There might have been another four or five.'

Adam was appalled.

'Was that in the film?' he asked.

'I think so. Anyway, it's well known.'

'Then why didn't you say so yesterday?' demanded Adam angrily. 'We should have looked. We should have hunted for the lair—'

'Oh, go on. We'd never have found it,' replied Richard calmly. 'It would have been like looking for a needle in a haystack.' Today he could defend himself, because he had no bad conscience about Foxy. A pretty job Adam would have made of looking after him, when all was said and done. 'And in any case,' he continued, 'if we had found any more, it would have been terribly complicated. It's going to be difficult enough hiding one.'

Adam looked at him broodingly in the ring of torchlight, and reminded himself to be furious with the Darkes, who had wanted the vixen dead, in the first place. It was a necessary reminder; he had been feeling far too kindly towards Richard, ever since morning.

'However,' Richard said, following his own line of thought, 'I do believe we'll manage it, and it's only till June, after all.'

For a day or two, they looked for little footprints in the red earth, and parted the long grass carefully along the sides of the croft paths as they walked, but no more Foxies were to be seen.

5 Down by the River

'Hey, guess what?' said Adam to Richard next day, when they met in the school yard after lunch. 'Remember what you were telling me yesterday about the Fauxes and their funny Weird? Well, this morning Puss was telling our class about it—local history, *she* says. I thought history was about what really happened. Anyway, she was very surprised to find that I knew all about it already—thinks I'm ignorant, does Puss.'

Puss was Mrs. Purves, Adam's teacher, known in the school as a most misleading woman. She had a jolly face, and looked like a bundle of fun, but she had the teaching technique of a heavy machine-gun.

'Well, fancy,' said Richard restrainedly. 'Did she tell you anything you didn't know?'

'She said the Fauxes used to live in your house. Is that right?'

'Yes. After they fell out with George II, they had to lie low for a bit, staying in the country and working their farms. They were quite poor for a while. They built our house about 1790, and lived there for a hundred years. Then some old Fauxe made a lot of money building steam ships on the Clyde, and when they got rich again, they built Garlet Place. After that, they began to let Fox Farm.'

'Why is the farm name spelled like an animal fox?' asked Adam.

'Because the people round here were all like you—couldn't spell for toffee,' retorted Richard.

'Ho, ho, ho,' said Adam, hollowly.

Then they dismissed the Fauxes from their minds,

because, for the time being, they had more pressing matters to think about.

During the next few days, the boys established a fox-care routine which seemed to work reasonably well, although they continued to feel like criminals every time they had to come away and leave Foxy alone in the deserted tower. Each morning, they took turns at running down, while the other covered the chores, to let Foxy out, and take him for a scamper through the bushes.

Adam had accepted this arrangement rather ungraciously, once it had dawned on him that Richard had no intention of doing all the work, leaving him at leisure to spend an hour alone with his fox. Adam was bitterly jealous of every minute Richard and Foxy spent together, but he could not make the unpleasant fuss he wanted to make; apart from his grudging, private admission that Richard had helped him far beyond what was reasonably required of him, he also needed the other boy's pocket money. And, in any case, when they got home from school at half-past three, and rushed down to the tower, there was no mistaking for whom Foxy reserved his warmest welcome. Adam could not understand why Richard showed no envy; when he had time to think the matter over, he came to the conclusion that he must really be very envious indeed, but was concealing his feelings, to deprive Adam of a triumph. So Adam did Richard an injustice, and triumphed furtively for a victory which existed only in his own imagination.

'I think these two have got a secret,' said Mrs. Darke indulgently to her husand, watching from the kitchen window as the two young figures disappeared into the mouth of the wood. 'My guess is that they're building a hut. Your tool bag has been up and down the road, and the wood pile seems to have gone down a bit.'

'Nice, if they're getting along together for a change,' said Mr. Darke, who occasionally wondered why Adam was at Fox Farm at all. Mainly, he supposed, because his wife, having started something, was not the sort of woman ever to turn back.

Every day, after lunch at school, the two boys made their way up the steep, cobbled Rivergate to Garlet Cross, where the shops marched in a neat square around the ancient Tolbooth tower, which had a clock like the moon, an onion-shaped roof, and a beautiful, flaunting weathercock. They bought minced beef, and sometimes a ham bone, prudently choosing to go to MacRae's butcher's shop rather than to Gillie's, which Mrs. Darke patronized. Richard could only too well imagine Gillie's large face, which seemed to take its colour and texture from his meat, thrusting across the counter, and his sing-song, inquisitive voice remarking, 'Weel, Mrs. Darke, thae wee laddies o' yourn ha' fairly gotten a taste fur ma mince. . . .' Then the fat would be in the fire, and a fine blaze there would be on account of it. So he and Adam went incognito to MacRae's, which had the additional merit of being cheaper. This was very important, for the daily provisioning of an animal was an expensive business, especially when, as well as meat, you also had to provide milk, and sometimes a small packet of chocolate drops for training purposes. These were intended as rewards for Foxy, for obeying commands such as, 'Sit!' and 'Heel!'; in fact, so far he seemed untrainable, which Adam said was because he was a fox, and Richard said was because he knew he could get the chocolate drops anyway, just by looking sweet.

One way and another, the week's pocket money was soon gone; by Wednesday they were dipping into the sugar bag, and into Richard's china pig with *A Present from Aberdeen* stamped in gold on its rump. By Friday, the pig, which had been casually fed with pennies and twopences, was losing weight rapidly, and Adam, who had more and cared more, was torn between his love of Foxy and his despair every time he had to put his hand into the sugar bag, and take out another fifty-pence piece. It was not that he grudged Foxy his food; he would have given Foxy anything. But this was his Australia money.

Several of the traps in the attic had caught mice, but Foxy quickly made it clear that he would have none of them; he snuffled suspiciously around the pathetic, broken-backed, bloodied little creatures which Adam hopefully distributed around his box, then turned away, his eyes fixed on Adam in a look of honeyed appeal. Adam sighed, and slapped some meat into the feeding basin, while Richard fetched a brush and shovel, and distastefully swept up the carcases.

'Spoiled,' he said tartly.

'I wonder,' said Adam thoughtfully. 'He's only a baby, after all. Maybe you ought to have skinned them. . . .'

On the Saturday after the arrival of Foxy in his life, Adam was to be alone in the afternoon. The Queen was paying a visit to Millkennet, and David and Richard, who were both Scouts, were to take part in a display of Youth Organizations at the Town Hall. Adam had resisted invitations to join the Scouts; now he resisted Mrs. Darke's invitation to go with her and her daughter Anne, who was a student nurse home for the week-end, to watch the Queen go by. He did not refuse rudely, he just refused, and Mrs. Darke, who was not as pressing with her invitations as she used to be, said he must please himself.

The Darkes went off in the van as soon as lunch was over,

David and Richard smart and shining in their Scout uniforms, Anne and her mother as carefully dressed as if they were going to shake hands with the Queen, instead of stand on the pavement at the corner of High Street, trying to catch a glimpse of her through the cracks in a fat policeman. Mr. Darke drove them, and Adam waved them off, noting that although the sky over Fox Farm was pale blue, and brushed with thin sunshine, over the distant spires and factory chimneys of Millkennet there lay a low, round cloud, like an enormous cushion of dark grey fur. Inevitably.

'Have you got your umbrella?' he bawled to Mrs. Darke above the revving of the engine.

She used it to wave to him, as the van bumped slowly up the lane, bouncing on the crumbly ruts until it reached the main road, where Mr. Darke changed gear, and rapidly increased his speed. Adam watched the van till it was only a blue spot far away on Garlet Hill, then he turned back into the kitchen to take some biscuits for Foxy from the tin on the dresser shelf. He took a large handful; if Mrs. Darke noticed, and commented, he would say that he had felt hungry, and taken them for himself. And if she complained, he would point out that his biscuits were paid for by the Social Work Department.

Adam could not tell why, suddenly, he felt aggressive and sore inside; the Darkes had asked him to go with them, after all, and would have been delighted if he had agreed. Yet somehow the sight of them going off like that, together, a family laughing and enjoying each other's company, made him feel painfully what they had, and he lacked. His pain made him furious, and he raged at himself savagely. For what had he to do with these Darkes, with their silly Scout uniforms, and their pink umbrellas, and their desire to look at the Queen? How dull their lives were, whereas he was going to Australia, to ride a horse, and herd sheep, in the Land of Opportunity. There he would grow strong, and tanned, and deep-chested, and be called Young Hew, to distinguish him from his strong, tanned, deep-chested father, in that great, wide open, sunrise and sunset land of Australia. Yet he had had so many unknown, unexpected emotions to contend with in the past week that he could not help feeling confused, and unlike his usual, single-minded self. He put the biscuits into his jerkin pocket, and went down through the wood, to be with Foxy.

The worship of the eager little animal was like balm, and Adam rejoiced in the prospect of having him all to himself for three hours. He put Foxy on the lead, and took him down the steep river bank on to the little patch of grey, shingly beach below the croft, where the greasy waters of the upper estuary, fast losing their tidal power, ebbed and flowed feebly over a few feet of dirty river bottom. Here it was safe to let Foxy run free; he could not climb the bank on one hand, and was properly suspicious of the water on the other.

Adam watched him as he gingerly explored the tide line, making little rushes at the water but never touching it, slipping and sitting down suddenly on the wet stones, trying to turn back the waves with shrill, imperious young barks. When he tired of this, he and Adam played; Adam thought it would be a great score over Richard if he could teach Foxy to come to heel while Richard was wasting his time doing gymnastics in Millkennet Town Hall. But it was not easy; Foxy came to heel smartly enough when there was a ginger biscuit as a reward, but as soon as the biscuits were gone he lost interest, and wanted to lie down on Adam's knees, and have Adam tickle his ears, and scratch his front.

Adam was pleased enough with this arrangement, for he was tired; for the first time in his life he was sleeping badly, always dozing and starting up in the darkness, imagining that he heard little cries of loneliness and distress, carried on the wind. Then he would lie awake, worrying, resenting Richard's even, peaceful breathing in the bunk below. So now he found a little shelter under the bank, rather like a little cave hewn out by the wind and rain in the soil, its shape held by a veining of exposed roots thrusting downward from the eaves of the little wood above. He crawled in, out of the wind, sitting with his back to the bank while Foxy spread himself like a rug over his knees, wrapping Adam's hand in his long, warm tongue.

'There now. Satisfied?' asked Adam.

Foxy agreed with a wink of his golden eye.

It was lovely to sit there peacefully, with your pet in your lap, or it would have been, if you had been able to push your worries to the back of your mind, and concentrate on the pleasure of the moment. Last Sunday afternoon, Adam had managed to do this, but now, it was no longer possible. Ever since last Sunday evening, when Richard, meaning to be comforting, had said, 'I do believe we'll manage it, and it's only till June, after all,' Adam had been in a state of increasing anxiety and insecurity. Of course, when he had found Foxy at the croft gate, he had only intended to keep him for a few weeks, until he was big enough to fend for himself. Then, one way or another, Adam would get rid of him, for it was not his purpose to have any creature hanging around indefinitely, infringing his freedom. But things had not worked out like that; from the very first moment when Foxy had chosen him, rather than handsome, clever Richard, as the one he would love best, Adam had responded with all the pent-up affection of his heart. He had very little experience of the give-and-take of loving; he did not know that when we love someone very much, the sorrow of knowing that one day we may lose him is part of the price we have to pay. Most people cope with this because they have more than one person to love. Now the fear of parting with Foxy broke upon Adam with the force of a storm. He realized the peculiar danger which lay in loving a fox. For a fox was a free creature of the wild that would follow its own instincts, and in three short months would be ready to hunt for itself. Then, in June, the cub would have left its mother; was it not possible that, however much he loved Adam *now*, then Foxy would leave him too?

With pain in his heart, Adam sat under the river bank, feeling Foxy's breathing vibrating intimately through his legs. It was quite warm and dry in the cave, with pale sunshine outside; away on his right, the cushion-cloud stood motionless, but now rain was beating down out of it on to royal Millkennet in a hard silver haze. Adam tried to smile at the thought of Mrs. Darke and Anne, huddling and muttering under the umbrella while the Queen splashed along Mill Street in her goldfish-bowl car, but nothing seemed funny today. If Foxy deserted him, Adam thought he would die of grief, and if Foxy deserted him, there was also the worry over what would be the effect on Foxy.

For if Foxy decided to return to the wild, where, Adam wondered miserably, could he possibly live? He would have to be taken right away from farms and houses and the haunts of human beings, if he were not to end like his mother, with a bullet through his heart. But where? Here, between the river and the plain, you might have thought that the country places ran on for miles and miles, but it was a river where fish were poisoned by industrial waste, and away on the western horizon the chimneys of Millkennet stood like upraised fingers, warning that this strip of unspoiled land was neighbour to an ugly sprawl of industrial towns, stretching right across the Central Lowlands, with factories, schools, cooling towers and power stations. Where, in all that, was there a place where a fox could be happy, safe and free?

Adam was roused from unpleasant meditation by the thrust of Foxy's nose into his sleeve. It was almost as if he knew what Adam was thinking, and wanted to reassure him. 'Don't be sad. I'll never leave you, Adam.' The little animal stretched, yawned, snuggled into his favourite place inside Adam's jacket, and fell asleep again. Adam felt comforted. Surely Foxy loved him too much ever to desert him.

Presently, they crawled out of the hole, and went further along the beach. Adam threw sticks, and Foxy danced after them, catching them in his mouth and worrying them ferociously. But he seemed unable to pick up the idea of bringing them back. Adam found a dead branch with twigs, snapped bits from it, and went on throwing automatically, while inside his head he began to torture himself with the other side of the problem.

For it was all very well, he realized, to say that he was sure Foxy would not desert him; if Foxy stayed with him, the difficulty of keeping him would be enormous. He could not stay in the tower room for ever. On the other hand, he could not stay anywhere else. However nice they might be, the hen-keeping Darkes would never tolerate even a tamed fox about the place, and try as he might not to, Adam could not help seeing their point of view. And even if Foxy could be kept clear of the henhouse, he was likely to have other bad, foxlike habits. Richard's story of the fox in the film, eating its way remorselessly through beds, bookcases and cars, was now a vivid reality to Adam, because already, it seemed, Foxy had begun to follow in the film-fox's foot-steps. On Wednesday, as a token of love, Adam had bought Foxy a yellow rubber ball to play with; by Thursday morning it had been gnawed into a mass of pulpy fragments on the tower room floor. Foxy's blanket, likewise, was now in shreds, and only yesterday afternoon, when Richard had laid down his anorak while he swept out the room, Foxy had got hold of it, and gleefully chewed a hole in its furry lining. Fortunately, it was on the inside, and so away from Mrs. Darke's eye, but it was a sign of foxiness, and could be a foretaste of trouble to come.

So was there no place in the world for a boy with a fox? Adam looked through a gap in the river bank, away across the plain to the north, where hills blocked the sky, showing black ribs through thin snow, as if someone had swept white paint across them with a careless brush. Then it occurred to him that he might run away, and take Foxy with him. They could take bedding and food, and make for the hills, find a real cave, and hide out there together. . . . It was tempting, but Adam knew that it would not work.

As soon as the Darkes found out that he was gone, they would telephone the police; cars and helicopters would be sent out, and long before he and Foxy had found a cave, they would be captured and brought back. Then there would be a terrible fuss; the Darkes would probably say that they couldn't be responsible for him any longer, and his social worker would come and take him away, back to the Children's Home which smelled of disinfectant and macaroni cheese. There was no place to hide in this tiny country, no hills high enough and lonely enough to conceal a child in care, whom nobody really wanted, but who wasn't allowed to run away if he didn't want anybody either. And as always, when he thought of the smallness of his native places, the vast spaces of Katoomba at sunset came into Adam's mind, and with the thought, a pang at his heart. For he had done what he had sworn never to do—let love of a creature come between him and his clearly planned future. His responsibility for Foxy meant that his dream of Australia could never be realized.

Adam sat on the dry shingle, with the great hills that were really so small on his right, and on his left the flouncing, shaggy body of grey water, flowing down from Millkennet, gateway to the concrete lands where no creature could ever be free. And then, as often when things seem as bad and hopeless as they can possibly be, he had an idea. Surely, he thought, it need not be a straight choice between Foxy and Australia. He could have both, if he turned for help to the only person he cared for, his own father. He told Foxy his plan, as he walked back to the tower, holding him on the lead now, for they were back in the wood, and night was beginning to close in.

'I'm going to write to my Dad in Australia,' he said, 'and tell him all about you and me. I'm sure if he knew the pickle we're in, he'd arrange for us to go out and stay with him, on the sheep ranch where he works. I don't suppose he'll mind having me a bit earlier than he intended when he hears about you. You'll have to be good, mind, and not start chewing up the sheep. But, then, I don't expect you'll want to, will you? There'll be miles and miles of open country for you to run about in, and you'll know where to find me when you want to come home. Of course, you'll probably have to go into quarantine for a few weeks when we get there, but you won't mind that—not when you know what a marvellous life we're going to have together afterwards. What do you say to that, then?'

Foxy said nothing, but looked quizzical. Any plan of

Adam's was good enough for him. Adam took heart from the fact that, for once, Foxy did not cry when he left him, but jumped into his box, and peeped over the edge, apparently satisfied that all their problems would be solved.

Adam walked back through the wood, listening to the day settling into night, watching the moon rise through a grid of branches, lonely and far away, with no other moon to keep it company. Now the family would be back, and in the warm kitchen he would hear what the Queen had been wearing, and how Richard had turned the most perfect cartwheel of his life under the Royal gaze, and how infuriating it was that the rain should have fallen on Mrs. Darke in her fur coat, and not on Adam in his old jerkin and denim jeans. And after tea, when they had all rushed into the sitting-room, to see if they were on the television News, he would slip away, and find paper and a pencil, and start composing the letter to his father.

6 *A Bad Horoscope*

Richard had been right in supposing that Adam did not care about anybody's troubles except his own. He did not. It was not, perhaps, surprising, in view of the kind of life he had had to lead, but it was certainly one of the least engaging things about him. When he saw poor Mrs. Fauxe in her pew in Garlet Church, sitting alone opposite the memorial to her family, he did not feel compassion, as Richard and David did, because now she had lost her only son too; he noticed what a big nose she had, and cared nothing for her troubles at all. And worse still, when trouble befell the Darkes, as it now did, he did not care very much about that either.

Richard had known that trouble was coming; he had hoped that by saying his prayers very fervently in bed at night, and trying not to think about the danger at any other time, he might somehow avert it. But things had perhaps gone too far. For two years, he knew, the croft had barely been paying its way; everything had gone wrong. Too much rain had blighted the potato crop, freak hailstorms had laid the barley flat in the field. A fox had broken into the hen-house, and the frost of last winter had lingered unkindly to nip the pears and apples at blossom time. The sudden drop in the market price of pigs had been the last straw, and Richard had been horrified, but not surprised one day to find in the sitting-room a newspaper, folded at the 'Situations Vacant' column, with a biro circle drawn round an advertisement stating that 'GLASGOW CITY PARKS DEPARTMENT has a vacancy for an EXPERIENCED GARDENER . . .' In the same paper, Richard had read his horoscope, predicting 'shortage of cash', 'change', and 'a long journey'. He noted these ill-omens gloomily, but managed to go on hoping that after all Father had not got around to applying for the job, and that somehow life would go on as usual in the place he loved. He said nothing about the advertisement to anyone, but he was at least a little prepared when the bomb dropped, which was after tea on the day after the Queen's visit to Millkennet.

Usually, after Sunday tea, the boys washed up, with David at the sink and Adam and Richard on drying, but today, before they could get up from the table, Mr. Darke cleared his throat, and said, 'Just a minute, lads. While Anne is still here, there's something I want to say to you.'

Richard watched the scene in terrified fascination, knowing what was coming, and also, now, that everyone else did too. Mr. Darke had not spoken once throughout the meal, except to say, 'Pass the butter, please,' and 'No more, thank you,' and Richard could tell by the sharp, etched look of his lined face that he was suffering because, in a moment, they were all going to have their fears confirmed. Without turning his eyes, Richard could see Anne's strong hands crumbling a piece of cake on her plate; David was like a pale statue.

Father spoke like someone delivering a carefully prepared statement, which he was. 'There's no easy way of telling you this, so I may as well come right out with it. Your mother and I have decided that we can't go on running the croft any longer, because it just isn't economic any more, and come another year we won't be able to feed and clothe you. I've been lucky enough to get a job without any trouble, the first I applied for. It's as Deputy Head Gardener with Glasgow Corporation—there's a flat goes with the job, and financially we'll be about twenty times better off than we are here, although—' his voice faltered momentarily, and his true feeling showed through his attempted cheerfulness '—I know that means as little to you as it does to me. I'm very sorry.'

Richard, who was sitting next to him, put out his foot, and hooked it round his father's leg in a friendly fashion.

David said, 'When?'

'September,' said Mr. Darke. 'That's when the present gardener retires, and for us, it's a good time. Gives us a few months to wind up here, and lets you finish the school year at your present schools.'

There was silence for a moment, of the kind in which every tiny sound is exaggerated into a nightmare noise, the clock ticking, a chair squeaking, the kettle boiling over with a hiss on the hot hob. Then David spoke again.

'Dad—is there no way?'

Mr. Darke shook his head.

'Unless there's a miracle between now and then—no, Davie. If it wasn't for the rent, we might manage, but by the time I've paid that every quarter, we're at rock bottom. We might have hung on for another year or two, by dipping into the little capital we have, but we have to think of the future. Mrs. Fauxe is old, and it doesn't look as if the young fellow is going to turn up now. That means that when the old lady goes, the property will be sold up. I'm a sitting tenant, and they couldn't put me out, but the one thing for sure is that the rent would double. Mother and I are agreed that we can't wait for that to happen. Hard as it is, we have to go. Now.'

It was kind Anne Darke, a rosy-faced girl of nineteen, who put her hand on Adam's shoulder as they left the kitchen, and said, 'Now don't let this upset *you*, Adam. You don't have to worry about a thing. You'll come to Glasgow with us—whatever happens, we'll always have a corner for you.'

Richard said nothing. When he rushed past Adam in the hall, his normally brown face an ugly fawnish colour, Adam knew he was only looking for a place to weep.

Which was too bad, of course, but Adam had his own problems, and writing the letter to his father was the most urgent of these. He would only have been distressed by the Darkes' trouble if it had threatened to separate him and Foxy, but he saw at once that, assuming the success of his plan, it did not. By September, he and Foxy would be in New South Wales, and neither would be haunted by the Darkes' memories of white blossom like snowfall on hawthorn hedges, the wind telling the poplars the news from the north, the changing colours of the plain, as the seasons turned, dying and coming again. Adam could say, 'It's sad,' but he could not really feel that it was so.

So while the young Darkes huddled together in David's room, trying to comfort each other and make the best of things, Adam went under his quilt with sheets of paper and a pen and a dictionary, and gave his attention to his precious letter.

He had been toiling over his task in every private moment he could snatch from chores and meals and going to church, since the previous evening; writing a letter was a very difficult thing for him to do. He wished he could ask Richard to check his spelling and punctuation, but that was out of the question, so he worked away with his school dictionary, looking up words, crossing out and writing and crossing out again. It was the first time he had ever regretted his inability to express himself on paper.

It wasn't because he thought it was really important, or that Hew, who was not himself much of a correspondent, would care. What Adam objected to was the idea that hateful Ruby might read the letter, and sneer at him to his father. Although of course, Adam reminded himself, exercising all a human being's power to believe only what he wants to believe, Hew had probably sent her packing long before now. No one could possibly stand five years in a house with Ruby. And if she was gone, then obviously Hew had only delayed writing to Adam because he was busy at the lambing, or the shearing, and was a bit slow at getting down to his writing pad at the best of times. And if that was so, this letter would be just what was needed to jog his elbow. . . . But still . . . Adam had his pride, and just in case Ruby should still be hanging around where she wasn't wanted, he was determined to write a perfect letter to his father.

On Monday, when Richard was in MacRae's shop, getting Foxy's dinner, Adam went into the post office, and bought one of the crackly, pale blue air-letter forms which he had seen Mrs. Darke use when she was writing to her sister in America. That night, he carefully copied his letter on to the form, and addressed it to 'Mr. A. Hewitt, Kent Farm, Targe Springs, N.S.W., Australia.' He knew the address because it had been written on a paper which he had once seen on his social worker's desk; he had memorized it, as something useful to know. Now he wrote it out slowly and lovingly, as if it were a magic spell. Next day he posted the letter, and settled down to wait for a reply. He did not expect it to come quickly; he had no idea how long mail took to reach Targe Springs from Garlet, but he supposed it would be a very long time, since only the other morning, on the radio, he had heard a man complain that it now took twice as long for a parcel to travel from London to Paris as it had done before the French Revolution. Adam was not good at geography, but he did know that Targe Springs was a lot farther from Garlet than Paris was.

It was a matter of some surprise to Richard that, after the announcement that his world was coming to an end, daily life should continue very much as if nothing had happened. But that was how it was; pigs must be fed and eggs collected, the van must go to market, seedboxes must be prepared for the last spring sowing they would ever do at Fox Farm. Richard went about his work as usual, following the familiar paths of a life which had been his for as long as he could remember, but he did it with a blackness of mind which overwhelmed him as he surfaced from sleep in the morning, and only left him as he drifted out into the other blackness of the night. For he hated the prospect of concrete pavements and a flat in the city with a deadly hatred, the more piercing because it had to be concealed, so that the other members of the family would not be upset by it. They were trying so very hard, and he must try too, but sometimes the very awareness of effort was the worst part of it.

When he was most unhappy, it was David's company that Richard sought, David's crooked-toothed grin which brought him relief from the alien, indifferent countenance of Adam Hewitt. He and David had always got along well enough together, although the difference in their ages prevented their being close friends; now common adversity drew them together, and Richard was grateful for David's patience, his kind promises of city treats—'There might even be advantages, Richie. You've never been to a Premier League football match, have you? You can come with me— and we might have a day at the Transport Museum.' Richard thanked him, but the boys did not look into each other's eyes, to see there the bleak knowledge of the shoddiness of all the city had to offer, the awareness that nothing in the world could ever compare with the staunch shelter of an ancient house, and the sound of great waters moving towards the sea.

As well as all of this, Richard had the continuing anxiety about Foxy, the deceit of keeping him at all, and the serious question of how much longer he and Adam could afford to feed him. Richard's personal troubles made him feel irritable and selfish; he was always tired, and he wished he could just be left in peace to grieve. But when he saw his father working in the field, patiently giving his best to the land that had failed him, and heard his mother making jokes with the milk boy from Fourwells, and remembered what this must be like for them, he felt deeply ashamed.

Mrs. Darke would have no grousing, or sulking; 'You have to remember,' she said robustly, 'how many people are far worse off than we are. Think of poor Mrs. Fauxe. Her husband was killed at El Alamein, then her younger boy died of polio in the Fifties. And now here's Robert gone too, and she's left alone in that awful mausoleum of a house. We've got far more than she has—we've got each other.'

Richard remembered this speech when he was speaking to Mrs. Fauxe a few days later.

It was on Thursday afternoon, after school, when Mrs. Darke had sent him along to Fourwells to pay the milk bill. The bicycle had a puncture, so he had to walk, and as he was coming out of the farm gate, on the way back, Mrs. Fauxe drew up in her grey Jaguar and offered him a lift. Richard opened the door, and climbed into the sumptuous, dog-scented interior; he felt some misgiving, for Mrs. Fauxe was a notorious driver, who had been down more ditches and up more telegraph poles than anyone else in the county. She had been to Court a few times, too, and it was reported that in her defence she had told the magistrate that there were far too many telegraph poles around—surely so many people didn't need telephones?—and that she was going to write to her M.P. about the urgent need to have the Garlet Road increased to twice its present width. This story, like the Weird, had probably gained much in the telling. Richard, however, did not like to refuse her offer, so he climbed in, taking care to fasten his seat-belt—Mrs. Fauxe was not wearing hers—and to keep a firm hold of the arm-rest on the side of the door. Mrs. Fauxe observed his precautions with a satirical eye.

'A belt and braces type, I see,' she remarked, letting in the clutch and launching into the twilight.

Richard watched her out of the side of his eye; her hawk-profile and raggy grey hair sprouting from under her tweed hat did not somehow invite remarks about the weather, and he did not know what else to mention. Mrs. Fauxe, however, seemed quite at home in silence, and soon drew up—safely, as it happened—at the end of Fox Farm lane.

'How's that brother of yours?' she asked in her sudden harsh voice, before Richard could thank her, and get out. She and David were both steeplechasing enthusiasts, and sometimes exchanged tips in the churchyard, much to the disapproval of Mrs. Darke, who said there was a place for everything.

'Oh, he's fine,' said Richard. 'He's busy working for his O-levels just now. He wants to be a doctor.'

'He's a good lad,' said Mrs. Fauxe, and Richard thought she sounded so wistful and lonely, despite her brusque manner, that he wanted to show her he cared. So he said, 'No word from Major Fauxe yet, I suppose, Mrs. Fauxe?'

'I'm afraid not yet, Richard.'

'Ah, well,' said Richard, becoming expansive because her voice had gone quiet, 'I expect it will take some time for news to get through, won't it? I mean—South America is such a very big country. I'm sure he's all right—I don't believe in the Weird a bit.'

This was a lie. Like everyone else in the district whom he knew, he believed in it fervently. After all, wasn't it in process of coming true?

However, it was the wrong thing to say. Mrs. Fauxe turned sharply in the driving seat and looked at him, energy seeming to drive out through her bright eyes in spikes into the gloom.

'Well, I should hope you do not!' she said vehemently. 'Weird, indeed! The Weird, as you call it, is nothing but a silly old wives' tale to frighten nitwits, and I hope you're none of such. I'm an old woman, and I don't believe in it, so how should you, a child of the space age? You might as well believe what you read in your horoscope. Now run along home, and ask your mother please to send me up a dozen of her brown eggs. My daughter-in-law is coming from London at the week-end, and Fox Farm eggs make the best omelettes.'

Richard scrambled out of the car and ran down the lane, terribly worried in case he had offended her. But when he turned at the corner of the yard, he could still see her sitting by the roadside, watching him. So he waved, and she waved back, and blew her horn in a friendly fashion.

'Mrs. Fauxe doesn't believe in the Weird,' Richard told his mother later, when they were together in the kitchen.

'She can't afford to, poor soul,' replied Mrs. Darke soberly.

But afterwards, Richard remembered that whether she did, or whether she did not believe in it, Mrs. Fauxe had taken the trouble to count back, and establish that her son Robert was thirteenth in descent from the Communion cup thief.

7 Sleeping Out

Now there was a change in the weather, bringing with it fresh anxiety about Foxy's welfare. For several weeks it had been alternately damp and mildly frosty, then for two days after the Queen's visit to Millkennet, rain had poured down over the whole plain, descending in blown curtains from a raggy sky. Grass and bracken were saturated, paths like a quagmire, the whole world a-drip. The boys had not liked to take Foxy out much, as they had no facilities for drying his wet coat; Foxy himself had been difficult, not wanting to go out, but behaving as if he were in a cage when he was kept in. On Tuesday morning, however, the boys felt a change in their toes even before they got out of bed; Richard was up first, and when he had scraped a spy-hole on the frost-encrusted window, he looked out on a landscape transformed. Every branch, every stone, every blade of grass was outlined individually with a feathering of silver rime, flushed pink by the low rays of a rising winter sun.

'Come and see this,' he said to Adam. 'It's beautiful.'

Adam came up groaning out of his cosy nest; he hated getting up in the morning. He tottered over to the window, clutching his striped pyjama jacket around his thin middle, and put a baleful eye to Richard's hole.

'Beautiful,' he said grimly, 'but too blasted cold. I hope poor little Foxy's all right.'

'Well, hurry up and get dressed, and you can find out,' said Richard, who already had his shirt and trousers on, and was pulling his jersey over his rumpled head. 'I'll sweep out the porkers for you, although I don't know why I'm so good to you, I really don't.'

Adam made no answer. He knew that Richard was good to him, but it was something he preferred not to acknowledge, even to himself, in case he might feel some obligation on his part to be good to Richard in return.

Outside, the world was wonderful, and Richard enjoyed it as he would enjoy everything now, with the thought at the back of his mind that he might be seeing it for the last time. Adam had no eyes for the things that Richard saw, the dark cobble-stones white-spiked into a pattern like checked tweed, delicate whorls chalked fuzzily on the crusty surface of the walls, a spider's web strung on the yard gate, its fluid lines stiffened into a shape of mysterious beauty. He rushed about his work, and as soon as he could, made off through the gap in the grey, frosted wall of the wood, plunging down among the dark trees, frantic to find out whether Foxy had taken harm from such agonizing cold. The frost had not penetrated the wood far enough to rime the inner trees; the ground and the bushes were dank and unadorned, but the chill was terrible, penetrating knife-like through his clothes.

It was hard to say how cold Foxy was; he was out of his box, and sniffing restlessly around the edges of the floor, but when he ran to Adam to be picked up and fondled, he was not actually shivering.

'Are you very cold, Foxikins?' Adam asked, letting him creep into his favourite place under the jerkin front. Foxy gave his stock reply to all the morning questions—two barks, affirmative or negative, depending on which answer the question seemed to invite.

Richard arrived in the doorway, red-nosed and anxious. 'What do you think?' he asked Adam.

'Hard to say. He doesn't seem to be actually shivering.'

The boys passed the little beast to and fro between them,

handling him and trying to assess how chilled he might be beneath his coat of fur.

'If only he has the sense to keep in his box, where it's warm,' Richard said. 'But it isn't likely—foxes are nocturnal, after all, and you can see from his puddles that he's been around a good lot during the night.'

Adam looked at him broodingly.

'I've been thinking,' he said. 'I'm going to start sleeping down here with him. He oughtn't to be left alone so much —it makes him so unhappy—and if I'm here, he can cuddle up with me, and we'll keep each other warm. Come on—I'll race you back to breakfast.'

Which was a convenient way, Richard realized, of ensuring that you were not contradicted; he was annoyed with Adam for assuming that he was going to contradict him, and for being right. For, with so much else on his mind, Richard felt strongly inclined to let Adam do as he liked and take the consequences, yet he also felt responsible for Adam, and for Foxy, and he knew that he would argue with Adam out of a sense of duty, when the time came. Richard felt a great weariness settle over him like a cloud; he was beginning to expect everything to end in disaster. Outside the tower door he found a stone, pretended it was Adam, and kicked it all the way back to the house.

The boys were not alone together again until after lunch, when they were going up Rivergate to the shops. Then, doing his duty, Richard said, 'Adam, you should think again. You really can't do this.'

Adam did not have to wonder what 'this' was. He had thought of nothing else all morning, and knew, in his cool way, that Richard had thought of nothing else either.

'I can,' he said, 'and I'm going to.'

Richard knew it was useless, but he plunged on.

'But Adam, think of the risk. Suppose Mother came into the room—'

'Richard, I've lived at your place for nearly two years, and in all that time your mother has *never* come into the room, except that one night when we had the light on late. She sleeps like the dead—she says so herself. Now listen, I know what I'm going to do. I'll wait until I hear everyone come up to bed, and give them time to fall asleep. Then I'll slip downstairs, and out through the pantry—half the time your Dad forgets to lock the door anyway. I'll borrow the alarm clock from Anne's room—'

'It might be missed.'

'Well, if it is, they'll think she's taken it back to the hospital,' said Adam impatiently. 'You've got to take some risks, for heaven's sake. I'll set it for six, then I can be back in the house before any of the rest of you are up.'

Richard fingered some marbles in his pocket, mused a while, and then changed tack.

'You'll get pneumonia.'

'No, I won't. I've thought that out too. There's a whole pile of camping equipment in the spare room. It belongs to David's school Camping Club, and they won't need it again till summer—I heard David say so. I'll borrow one of those Arctic sleeping-bags, and a couple of old blankets from the back of the airing cupboard. I'll sleep in the rowing boat. And I'll have Foxy. He's better than a hot-water bottle.'

It was all as Richard had expected.

They reached the Co-op Dairy, and went in to buy Foxy's daily half-pint of milk. When they came out, Richard played his last card.

'I could tell Mother.'

Adam looked at him with his sea-gull's eyes.

'But you won't,' he said.

It was not a threat, only a statement of belief. And Richard knew he wouldn't, although all but one of his senses told him that he should.

Becoming involved, as usual, against his better judgement, Richard went upstairs with Adam after tea, and helped him to bundle all the things he needed into an old rucksack of his father's. The hoar frost, which had melted during the day under a joyless sun, began to form again after dark; the cobbles in the yard and the roof of the sty glittered in the moonlight in millions of sharp little sparks.

'It's going to be just as cold as last night,' warned Richard, as he stuffed an old checked travelling rug in on top of the bunchy, breathing feather sleeping-bag.

'It couldn't be colder anywhere than it is in here,' pointed out Adam, shivering in their unheated room. 'It would be a laugh if you died of hypothermia in the night, while I was tucked up cosy in the rowing boat.'

'You would laugh,' said Richard wearily.

By common consent, they kept apart till bed time, each finding the company of the other an irritant. At half-past eight, they had bowls of cornflakes for supper, and at ten to nine they went upstairs to get ready for bed. Through the floor, they could hear the self-important, booming little tune which heralded the nine o'clock television News. While Adam was in the bathroom, gently wiping the parts of himself that showed with a warm flannel, he heard Richard slip downstairs again; he was gone for some time, and Adam was in bed before he reappeared, stealthily, holding something inside his dressing gown. It was a thermos flask.

'I made you some soup,' he said. 'I knew the coast would be clear while the News was on. Tomato—it's one of those individual packets David has for when he goes orienteering.

We must buy a box tomorrow—you really must have something hot, sleeping out in this weather.'

He knelt down, and pushed the flask under the flap of the rucksack. Adam did not thank him; to his rage and embarrassment, he felt his face flushing scarlet with a mixture of pleasure, gratitude and guilt. It was the first time he ever acknowledged to himself that Richard was the best kind of friend a boy could possibly have, one who might disapprove of every single thing you did, yet backed you up, and really cared what happened to you.

'I shouldn't have dragged you into all this,' he said hoarsely, lying down and covering his head with the blankets. Through a chink, he watched Richard's bare feet pass him, going up the ladder to the top bunk.

'You didn't drag me,' said Richard calmly. 'I wanted to help. He's a nice little fox. It's your turn to put off the light.'

Then Adam saw that he had been wrong about Richard. The other boy was not jealous. He was fond of Foxy, but did not mind that Foxy preferred Adam. This was a puzzle to Adam; he did not know, and Richard could not have told him, that the reason was that Richard had many other people to love.

Richard fell asleep within ten minutes. Warmth seeped into his cold body from his hot-water bottle, spreading into every corner, then he grew pleasantly drowsy, then he was asleep. It had been so with Adam until Foxy came; then his habit was disturbed, and tonight, so taut and expectant was he that he could not possibly have spoiled his plan by dropping into sleep. With peeled ears, like a fox, he lay under his blankets, hearing beyond Richard's regular breathing all the late evening sounds of the house, the familiar tune bouncing out of the television set at the end of the News, the grinding of bolts as the front door was locked, the running of water in the bathroom, the clock whirring rheumatically and striking ten. The Darkes normally went to bed early, as they had to be up at the crack of dawn next morning; Adam heard David coming up, then his father, their weight making the old stairs protest tiredly. Mrs. Darke was last; she would be preparing vegetables for tomorrow's broth, or reading some article on the newspaper she was using to wrap up the peelings. The clock had struck eleven before she came up too, and Adam knew he must allow a while for her to undress, put in her curlers, tell her unwilling husband what she had been reading in the paper, and fall asleep herself. To be on the safe side, he let twelve strike before, cautiously, he crept out of bed, and began to put on his clothes, two pairs of socks, two jerseys, his jerkin and the striped woolly hat which Anne had knitted for him at Christmas. He had reconnoitred the stair when he came home from school, pinpointing the places where the creaks came; now he slipped down noiselessly, treading on the outer edges of the steps, missing out the most treacherous ones. In the moonlit kitchen he sat down to put on his boots, then, slinging the rucksack across his shoulder, he opened the pantry door and stepped out into the yard.

Coming straight from bed, he felt the cold take his breath away. The moon was riding high and cold in a sky made blacker by the contrast of white stars thrown in handfuls across it, and as he scuttled across the yard, accompanied by his tiny moonshadow, like a humpy-backed dwarf, for the first time Adam felt a little tremor run through him, not of fear, exactly, but a thrill because the world of the night, unlike the world of the day, was so vast and enigmatic. He was swallowed into the throat of the wood, and the dwarf at his side disappeared. The darkness was absolute; he had to stop, and find his torch, before he could see the path at all.

Some people talk, unaware, about the silence of the night. Now, as he glided along through the trees, stepping always into the yellow circle of light which the torch cast in front of him, Adam realized that night was not silent at all. It was full of its own sounds, small and intimate, rustlings and breathings and purrings which came to him from the hidden nightlife of birds and plants and tiny beasts, who might have revealed themselves, had they not been scared by the sound of a giant blundering past. The trees went by in the beam, knobbly white pillars with swathes of black velvet in between, and an owl hooted, low and admonitory, somewhere above Adam's head. Richard would have been scared out of his wits, imagining nameless frights lurking in every shadow, but Adam was happy; perhaps he had feared reality too much to be afraid of the invisible. The crumbly wall of the tower reared up suddenly, the warped door picked out by the torch; he pushed it open and directed the beam down the narrow stone passage, built so that men with swords could only go through one at a time. So long ago, so long forgotten. Adam squeezed through, the rucksack bumping and scraping on the stone.

'Foxy,' he said. 'Come on, boy. Come on, Foxy!'

Foxy was out of his box, nosing around the trestle table, prowling. He turned round on himself as Adam came in, his ears going up, his eyes like green-gold reflectors in the unexpected light. He stood for a moment, as if he could scarcely believe that Adam was real, then he ran to him, not barking joyfully and wagging his tail, but crying quietly, his thin body quivering with love and delight.

Adam sat down on the rucksack, and gathered the little creature into his arms; he buried his face on Foxy's neck, smelling his warm animal scent, and knew a moment of pure happiness as the warm tongue slapped his ear, and began to explore his neck, pushing in between his collar and his hair.

'I'm going to sleep here with you,' Adam told him, 'every night from now on, until we leave for Australia. You won't be cold and lonely any more. Now just wait till I make the bed, then we'll get into it together.'

He got up, and tweaked the tarpaulin off the rowing boat, an old, flat-bottomed craft with *Dragonfly* painted on her stern. He put the duckboard in the bottom, and spread out the feather sleeping-bag, and the blankets. Then he gave the astonished Foxy a leg up, and climbed up after him, fully clothed, into bed.

'Now, listen you,' he said warningly to Foxy, as he set the alarm clock for six, and uncorked the hot, savoury tomato soup, 'you're not to eat the bedclothes. Understand? The Camping Club wouldn't like it, and neither would I.'

Foxy looked pained, as if such an idea would never have entered his head. He backed tail-first into the sleeping-bag, and settled himself with his head on Adam's chest, giving little shivers of bliss.

Adam drank Richard's soup by torchlight, watching the fluent shadows of the round chamber weaving about his head. He could feel the warmth trickling down his body, bringing him sleep. When he had finished, he put out the light, and when he had made sure that Foxy was warmly tucked into the blankets, he put his arm over him, and fell asleep.

8 *A Financial Crisis*

For the rest of the week, Adam was jubilant, and even Richard, who had got into the habit of expecting that punishment for Adam's sins would fall on him at any minute, had to admit that everything seemed to be going along reasonably well. Certainly, Foxy was happier; he scarcely complained at all now when they had to leave him alone for spells, and sleeping out did not seem to be doing Adam any harm, apart from occasional attacks of chilblains. His nightly routine remained mercifully unsuspected by the grown-ups, who only noticed with pleasure that the boy suddenly seemed more relaxed, helpful, friendly, even.

'I do believe that boy is beginning to settle down at last,' remarked Mrs. Darke to her husband one evening, when Adam and Richard had gone out of the kitchen, laughing helplessly over some silly joke. 'I'd be so thankful if he'd make up his mind that he wanted to stay with us, and let us make some more permanent arrangement.'

Mr. Darke looked at her over the edge of the *Gardener's Weekly*, almost surprised by the yearning in her voice.

'That's up to him now, Mary, surely,' he replied. 'You've done all you possibly could, and more.'

Mrs. Darke sighed, and turned to open the oven door a fraction, to check on the health of a pudding she was baking.

'Maybe,' she said, coming back to the table, 'but—I can't help worrying, Dick. As things are now, he could be taken away from us at any time. Even that wretched man in Australia has more claim to him than we have.'

Mr. Darke knocked out his pipe on the brick lining of the chimney, and looked cynical.

'I don't think you should waste your time worrying about him,' he told her. 'If he'd been a man at all—'

'Yes, I know. All I'm trying to say is that the boy is at risk, as long as we don't have any legal right where he's concerned. And if he were taken away from us, he'd care more than he knows. He's been hurt so much already—that's what makes him shy away from people. He can't trust anybody.'

Meanwhile, Adam was happy with Foxy, happier than he could ever have imagined possible, knowing that soon he would be going to Australia, and would never come back to Scotland as long as he lived. He was even prepared, in his new-found feeling of well-being, to put out some rays of warmth to the people around him, which they misinterpreted, believing, like him, what they wanted to believe.

But every silver lining, as Mrs. Darke was wont to say, has a cloud. Foxy was proving very expensive indeed to feed. Richard said he was greedy, and Adam said he was a growing lad, but whichever was true, he ate his way through thirty pence-worth of meat every day, drank half a pint of milk, and was always ready to accept a chocolate drop, or share a biscuit, whenever Richard and Adam came down to the tower. Certainly, such feeding was doing him good; his skinny body was rounding out, and his coat acquiring a silky surface, as if he were washed with a very expensive shampoo. But Adam's early estimate of a pound a week to feed him had been wide of the mark; his and Richard's combined pocket money was disposed of on Monday, and for the rest of the week they had to dip into rapidly dwindling capital.

For a while, the boys made a determined effort to interest Foxy in the kind of food which was always considered a treat at the pigsty, crusts and carrot tops, plate scrapings and porridge, but Foxy had been indulged from the first; he thought as little of this fare as he had of the mice. Then Adam would claim to hear his tummy rumbling with hunger in the night, and next day they were back to buying beef at MacRae's. Now Adam regretted heartily his early extravagances, the yellow ball, a blue enamelled dish, a fine red leather collar which he had bought in the first flush of gratitude for Foxy's affection; the Aberdeen piggy bank, through no fault of Richard's, could no longer raise a jingle, and Adam had stopped worrying about arriving destitute in New South Wales. Now his only concern was how much longer he could afford to feed Foxy; he rather wished he had had the foresight, in his letter to Australia, to ask for a few pounds on loan. His father would not have grudged him the money, he thought, conveniently forgetting that he was where he was because his father would not send a few pounds each month to Aunt Nancy for his maintenance. Adam had now so firmly convinced himself that his father would prove to be the strong, generous rescuer of himself and Foxy, that he had completely obliterated all the betrayals and unpleasantness from his mind.

'We must plan in advance,' said Adam to Richard, as they were walking back to school from MacRae's, under a small white sun. 'We should have something in mind, before the money runs out completely. My father always used to say that you should look ahead, and know what you were going to do before the crisis came.'

His father had never said anything of the sort, but Adam liked to quote him as an authority. He had invented so many opinions and wise sayings for Hew over the years, that he had now actually come to believe that Hew had said them. They made the man seem more real, yet, since they were untrue, in fact made him less so.

'It's my fault,' said Richard unhappily. 'I've hardly contributed anything.'

There was a time when Adam would have encouraged such self-accusation; making Richard feel guilty and watching him suffer had long been one of his amusements. But since he had been sleeping out with Foxy, and Richard had shown his concern by filling the thermos flask every night with hot soup, their relationship had changed. Adam was pleased and grateful, a new experience for him.

'It's not your fault at all,' he said now. 'You haven't got any money because you're always buying presents for people. If I have some, it's because I've been a miser. Anyway, we're not at the last gasp yet—let's think for a bit, and see what we can come up with. There's bound to be some way of getting cash, if only we can think of it.'

When Adam spoke to him like this, Richard felt absurdly happy, as if the sun had suddenly turned gold and summery, and warmed him right through. He leaped up the school stair light-heartedly, and entered the class room whistling, only to be brought right down to earth again by a scolding.

Nonetheless, he was very anxious to help. He knew that the supply of money was going to run out long before June, and that when it did, Adam would do something desperate; there was a recklessness about him which belongs only to those who have little or nothing to lose. All the afternoon, while he wrote notes on the Industrial Revolution, and painted a very black picture of women and children toiling down in a coal mine, Richard's mind was busy with quite different affairs, and by the time when the bell rang at three o'clock, he had decided what to do. He would follow his instinct, which in time of trouble was exactly the same as Adam's; he would go to his father.

Never in all his life would Richard hate doing anything more than he hated what he was planning to do now. To ask his father for money at a time when the croft was folding up for lack of it, seemed to him almost unforgivable, yet this evil must be balanced against the other evil of letting Foxy starve, and driving Adam, who was at last beginning to trust him, to some disastrous course of action. Adam would do something crazy, and the next thing to happen would be that Miss Whatshername from the Social Work Department in Glasgow would come and take him away. That must not happen. Some day, perhaps, Richard thought, he could explain and apologize to Father, but Adam would be beyond explanations and apologies—if he were not helped now.

So that night after tea, when Mr. Darke had gone into the sitting-room to read the newspaper before the television News came on, Richard followed him, and sat down opposite him in one of the sagging, baggy leather armchairs which Mrs. Darke had always said she would replace one day, when pigs could fly. He did not speak, but stared hard at the outside of the newspaper till Mr. Darke grew uncomfortable, and fidgeted, and put the paper down. He looked at Richard over his glasses, which were mended in two places with Sellotape, because he was always sitting down on them by mistake, and said, 'Is there something I can do for you? Or are you only here for a free read?'

'There's a matter,' said Richard formally, 'I want to discuss with you.'

'Eh? A matter? What's that?'

'Pocket money,' said Richard firmly.

'Pocket money?'

'Yes. Adam and I have talked it over, and we don't think twenty-five pence a week is enough. This is a time of inflation, you must remember, and we haven't had a rise for two years.'

As he heard the words come out, Richard hated himself; he knew this *was* unforgivable. But to his surprise Mr. Darke smiled, though he answered seriously enough.

'It's a time of inflation for me too,' he pointed out. 'I just don't seem able to persuade my pigs to put on weight, or my hens to lay more eggs, because it's a time of inflation. I really don't think I can afford to give you any more at the moment.'

Feeling a worm, Richard pressed his case.

'David gets a pound,' he pointed out.

'Yes, I know. David is older. Out of the pound he puts something in the Savings Bank, and pays his School Club subscriptions, and bus fares if he has to go back to Millkennet in the evening. You don't have any expenses like that. I'll be raising Adam's money when we move to Glasgow, and he starts Secondary School, but I'm afraid you'll have to wait a while longer, my son.'

Richard looked so crestfallen that his father felt sorry for him.

'Do you need the money for something special?' he asked gently.

The question made Richard nervous. He felt he was taking a risk in answering it, but trusting to his father's innocence of what was going on, and respect for his privacy, he said cautiously, 'Well, yes, in a way. But it's a secret something, Dad.'

Mr. Darke grinned at him. He liked Richard as a person, apart from loving him as a son.

'I dare say we can contribute to a secret something,' he said, and getting to his feet, walked across the floor in his old slippers to the writing bureau where he kept his cash box, along with all the bills and papers relating to the business of the croft. He opened the box with a little key, took out two pound notes, and handed them to Richard.

'One for Adam, one for you,' he said. 'Don't spend it all on riotous living.'

Then Richard, looking through tears at his father's good-natured, weatherbeaten face, where lines of anxiety contended with lines of humour, felt an overwhelming, anguished desire to tell him everything, about the fox in the tower, and the cost of feeding him, and Adam's sleeping out in the rowing boat in the middle of winter; it would have been such a relief to let it all come pouring out, so that Father could take the responsibility, and decide what was best to do. But he could not. If he betrayed Adam now, Adam would never trust him—or anyone else again, as long as he lived. For a while longer, he must deceive Father, and be faithful to Adam. If Richard had known that Adam had written to *his* father, telling the secret and asking for help, while denying him the same privilege, he would have been very angry indeed, but deep down, he would have understood.

He screwed up his eyes to dry them, put the money in his pocket, and said, 'Well, thanks very much, Dad. You're a pal. That'll be a big help. Hey look—it's time you had the telly on. It's a minute to six.'

Later on, when they were going to bed, Richard told Adam what had happened, and gave him the two pound notes to put in his sugar bag, beside the few remaining fifty-pence pieces.

'I thought it was worth a try,' he said. 'I'm sorry it didn't come to much.'

'It came to a great deal,' said Adam warmly, taking out

the blue paper bag and stuffing away the precious green and white notes. 'Don't be daft, Richard—it's eight weeks pocket money for either of us, and it'll buy Foxy a load of food. It's better than an increase, I reckon—we wouldn't have got more than ten pence each, at best, and that really wouldn't have made much difference. I think you've done a good job, my lad. Puss would be proud of you. Take a gold star and go to the top of the class.' But he paused, in the midst of laughter, his smooth white forehead wrinkling momentarily into a frown. Then he added, 'It seems mean, though, doesn't it—taking money from your Dad, under the circumstances.'

Which proved how far a person could travel on the road from self-concern, in rather less than three weeks.

Again, Richard basked in the warmth of Adam's praise like a kitten in the sun. He turned a couple of somersaults on the top bunk, and slithered down between the sheets. Then he made a remark, casually, as one does, without ever supposing that one may live to regret it.

'All the same, I wish I had something worth selling,' he said.

9 *The Microscope*

As the hoard of fifty-pence pieces dwindled still further, and Foxy still refused any of the cheaper kinds of food which the boys tried to give him, and still no letter came from Australia, Adam remembered Richard's words, and the tiny seed of an idea, so planted, quickly grew to a tree. Furtively, he began to cast his eye around the house, wondering whether there was anything there that he might steal. For he also remembered that there was a second-hand shop in Millkennet: 'Harold P. Hardy, Auctioneer and Second-Hand Salesman'; the boys passed it often on the way to the Swimming Baths, a dingy shop with dirty windows and a withered pot plant in the doorway. No one would know Adam there, he thought, and he could sell—well, something—without any awkward questions being asked, and the money would ensure that he and Foxy could be together for a little longer. For that was what it had come to, now; all the varied interests of life had narrowed to this one, vital concern, how to keep Foxy in food for the next week, the next day—and what was to be done when all the money was gone. Adam's attitude towards stealing was a confused one. He was not really dishonest by nature, and he would never have thought of stealing for himself. On the other hand, he would cheerfully have stolen—or worse, have egged Richard on to steal—bags of minced beef from the freezer, partly because he considered anything justified when it was for Foxy's benefit, and partly because he did not, at that time, care enough for the Darkes to feel any pricks in his conscience because he might be harming them.

He had never actually stolen anything, and he did not

want to steal now, especially from the Darkes who, he admitted in his new mellow mood, had been so good to him. This made a small awkwardness, yet when it came to a choice, there was still no doubt in Adam's mind as to whose interest came first. He liked the Darkes, but Foxy was his passion; he was perfectly sure that it was his duty to support and protect Foxy, by every means possible, Foxy who was in danger of his life, till the letter from his father came. Then all would be put to rights; later on, he comforted himself, the Darkes could be repaid. It would really only be borrowing, not stealing at all.

So he looked around, but he could see nothing. The Darkes had very little that was valuable, and what they had tended to be too big; Adam could not lift the grandfather clock, or the piano, and run off with it under his jacket. He knew that he must look for something small, something which, with any luck, would not be missed for a while, preferably not till he was safely *en route* for Australia. But since the only possible small things were Mrs. Darke's watch and garnet brooch, and Mr. Darke's gold cuff-links, which were worn quite frequently, he was on the verge of giving up the idea, when one day Richard came into their bedroom looking very hot and indignant.

'It's not fair of David,' he burst out angrily. 'He won't ever lend me anything.'

'What won't he lend you?' inquired Adam, who always enjoyed Richard in a temper, with his brown eyes snapping and his face the colour of a rooster's comb.

'His microscope. I wanted to take it to school, so that our class could look through it at the moulds we've been growing on different materials, but the mean beast won't let me. Says it cost thirty pounds and I might break it. As if I was stupid. And it's not as if he uses it very much. It lies at the back of his cupboard for months on end, and I don't think he even remembers it's there.'

This was the most interesting information which had come Adam's way for a long time, and he listened with pricked ears. But when he spoke, he tried to sound very casual.

'Where on earth did he get thirty pounds to buy a microscope?' he asked, pretending to be very busy making his bed.

'He didn't,' growled Richard. 'Granny gave it to him for his birthday—something to do with one of his fads, I forget which. You know he's her favourite—he only has to mention that he wants something, and she runs out and buys it for him. Mother says she must have more money than sense.'

Adam agreed with Mother; one of the things he and Mrs. Darke had in common was that they both had more sense than money, even if much of Adam's sense had temporarily deserted him. He kept this conversation with Richard in mind; when the time came, he would not so much mind stealing from David, with whom he was only on slight terms of friendship.

The time came the following Saturday. The money was obviously going to run out during the next week, and Saturday was the only day when the boys could go to Millkennet, because on week days the shops would have been closing by the time they reached them, after school. Things were made easier for Adam, too, by the fact that Richard was going on an outing with his teacher to a nearby castle; he set off after breakfast, with his haversack over his shoulder, tramping through fine rain up the croft road to meet the minibus which was collecting children from the outlying farms and cottages. He was looking forward to the trip enormously, and had, he kept assuring himself, shaken off his cares for the day. He was going to have a good time, and sing songs in the bus, and drink lemonade, and generally try to forget that there was a fox locked up in the tower, and that he had a foster-brother who had not spent a night in his own bed for a fortnight. If Mother found out . . . but there, he was beginning to worry again. Forget it, he ordered himself, as the minibus hove into sight, looking like a Matchbox toy far away on the road from Hutchinsneuk. Forget it. Worry tomorrow. Nothing terrible is going to happen today. The minibus got larger, arrived, and stopped while he got in. The doors closed, and they drove off; most of the passengers were drinking lemonade and striking up songs already. As the bus got to the Garlet turning, Richard looked back, and saw the house, and the poplars, and the grey head of Fox Tower sticking up out of its ruff of unleaved trees. He sighed, and tried to concentrate on the business of enjoying himself.

With Richard safely out of the way, Adam was pleased to discover that other things were in his favour too. After breakfast, David announced that he was going to spend the day at Garlet with his friend Angus, and would not be back till four o'clock, and it turned out that Mr. and Mrs. Darke were not going to Millkennet to shop, as they usually did, because Mr. Darke had to go to Glasgow, to a meeting of the Farmers' Union.

When he was helping her to wash up, and tidy the kitchen, Adam said to Mrs. Darke, 'Would you mind if I went into Millkennet this afternoon? I want to go to the library to look for a book on seals. I have a project to do.'

It was not a lie; funny, how he prided himself on not being a liar, even though he was about to become a thief.

'Of course I wouldn't mind,' said Mrs. Darke, delighted

to hear Adam mentioning words like 'project' and 'library'. She had always been convinced that he could do really well at school, if only he would settle down to work, and show some interest. 'But how will you get there? I have my baking to do, but I could run you as far as Garlet in the van.'

'Oh, no, thanks,' replied Adam hastily. He had no desire to sit beside Mrs. Darke all the way to Garlet Cross, holding her son's stolen microscope in his lap. 'I don't want to bother you. I'll take the bike as far as Garlet, and chain it up in the school shed. I can go in by bus from Rivergate.'

'Yes, all right,' agreed Mrs. Darke. She believed in encouraging children to be independent. 'Only be back before it's dark, please—I don't want you cycling over that road alone, after nightfall.'

She said it half lovingly, half severely, in just the way a mother would speak to her own child, Adam thought. In spite of himself, he felt warmed by her concern, and sad that in so short a time he would have left her, never to return. His resolve to go did not waver, but neither did he do as he would have done a month ago, and arm himself against his own feelings by telling himself that she was only anxious because, if any harm came to him, she would be in trouble with the Social Work Department. He promised that he would catch the four o'clock bus from Millkennet, and be back at Fox Farm by five.

'We'll have an early lunch, if it's just to be you and me,' said Mrs. Darke, 'then I'll get on with my baking, and you can be up at Garlet in time for the one o'clock bus.'

And so they parted, she to run her husband, looking very strange and Sunday-ish in a dark suit, with a shirt and tie, to Hutchinsneuk Station, to catch the Glasgow train, and he to sit in his bedroom, waiting for the coast to be clear, so that he could take the microscope.

Always, afterwards, Adam believed that he had been slightly out of his mind that day, as if his anxiety about Foxy, and his own future, had changed him for the time being into another kind of person. For this was a criminal act, in no way to be compared with helping oneself to a few bags of minced beef; yet neither fear nor conscience troubled him, and he went about his task with a cold detachment, almost as if he were observing someone else doing things which normally he would never have done in a thousand years.

As soon as he heard the van back out of the stable, jolt across the lumpy cobbles, and begin to crawl in second gear up the rutted track to the road, he got up, went next door to David's room, and opened his cupboard. David's tidiness was unnerving; everything was ranged on the shelves with incredible precision, his school books and note-books at the top, his geology equipment one shelf down, rugby and gym gear below that, and so on. At the very bottom of the cupboard, actually on the floor, were a box of slides, a rack of test tubes, some rubber tubing, like thin red snakes, and a bunsen burner. Behind these, against the cupboard wall, and well out of the view of anyone not actually looking for it, was the microscope, in a polished wooden box. Adam undid the little curly hook, and opened the box; the microscope lay bedded on green baize, a shining instrument of brass and glass, looking very valuable.

Thirty pounds, Adam thought, in awe. Of course, he wouldn't get thirty pounds for it, but he might get fifteen. He would ask for twenty. He pushed the slide box across the space where the microscope had been, rearranged the rubber tubing, and closed the cupboard. He went back to his own room, wrapped the box in a piece of brown paper, and took it straight down to the stable with his library book, stowing them both away in the saddle-bag of the bicycle, before Mrs. Darke came back. Then he went down to the tower, to play with Foxy. They scrambled down to the beach again, and played with the remains of the yellow ball, and Adam was cool and hard and happy, as if he didn't know the difference between right and wrong.

'Everything's going to be fine now,' he said to Foxy, fondling the animal's delicate ears and enjoying his warm breath on his wrists. 'You don't have to worry now, old Fox. By tonight, I'll have plenty of money to feed you, and as soon as that letter comes from my Dad—Australia, here we come.'

Foxy stuck his whiskery muzzle into the palms of Adam's hands, and agreed with every word he said, looking up at him with uncritical adoration.

His own moral indifference sustained Adam through lunch; it would have been a very uncomfortable meal if he had really been able to take in the fact that he had stolen a valuable microscope, that the basic, criminal act had already been committed by him. Warmed by Scotch broth and Mrs. Darke's easy company, he became quite expansive, and told her all about the Children's Home in Glasgow, and the terrible macaroni cheese, and the Matron, whose real name was Mrs. Thorpe, but who was known to all and sundry as Captain Hook. He imitated Captain Hook, pulling hideous faces; Mrs. Darke laughed, and said that if she was really like that, she must be a cross between Dracula and Mickey Mouse, and certainly shouldn't be in charge of a Children's Home.

When they had finished, Adam put on his waterproof, got out the bicycle, and cycled off up the Garlet Road, while Mrs. Darke began quite light-heartedly to clear the table, ready for baking. Every day she felt more certain that Adam was at last allowing himself to become an established member of the family, and she wondered whether perhaps the news of the move to Glasgow had anything to do with his change of heart. He was a city-bred boy, after all; perhaps he disliked country life, and country pastimes. If so, thought Mrs. Darke, it simply proved the truth of the saying that only an ill wind blew nobody any good; it would be comforting to think that something worthwhile had resulted from so much failure and heart-break.

It was not very far from Garlet to Millkennet; Adam caught the bus without delay, and was soon being trundled over flat, uninteresting roads which ran through what was neither town nor country, but rather the untidy edges of one town reaching out to touch the untidy edges of another. There was grassland, with some trees, but always spotted with garages and Council houses and factory buildings; long before the bus reached the centre of the town, it met the outskirts of Millkennet, crawling out over what had only a generation ago been open country, overlaying green with grey. To see the view at all, Adam had to wipe a peep-hole with his glove on the breath-misted window of the bus, and peer past clinging raindrops on the outside; he only bothered to do it once, for this was the landscape which depressed him most, the half rural, half urban desert where wild things could live, but every minute in peril of their lives. He let the glass haze over again, and sat motionless in the foggy grey interior, clutching the box and his library book under the breast-flap of his waterproof. Soon streets folded in upon him, darkening the windows, shops overhung by offices and dwelling houses, an unlovely mixture of grimy nineteenth century stone and raw modern glass and concrete. Adam got out of the bus at the War Memorial, and walked down Kennet Street to the library, through wind-tossed rain.

It was now a really horrible afternoon, and Adam was glad to find shelter, and the sudden comfort of central heating in the Children's Room. He spent nearly an hour there, sitting at a little table, surrounded by books about seals, and foxes, and with the little brown paper parcel containing the microscope placed firmly before his eyes. If he got up to fetch a book, or return one to its place on the shelf, he watched the parcel out of the side of his eye all the time— foolishly nervous, since, apart from the librarian and a tiny girl looking at a picture book, there was no one else in sight.

It was after half-past two when Adam realized that he was reluctant to leave the library; he had selected the best book for his project, had glanced at lots of others, and now found himself looking with great concentration at a model railway catalogue, which was strange, since he was not in the least interested in model railways. He told himself that he didn't want to go out of the cosy, pleasantly lit library into the cold wet street; outside the sky was almost dark between the roofs of the buildings in Church Street, and the wind was spattering rain like handfuls of dried peas against the windows of the Children's Room. But the truth had nothing to do with the weather; now that the moment had actually come when he must walk up the street again, past the War Memorial and the Swimming Baths, turn the corner at the police station and enter Hardy's second-hand shop, Adam was afraid. Sitting at the table with the parcel in front of him, he would not at first admit that he was afraid, then, when he did, he was furious, and abused himself roundly for being so stupid. For he had gone over all this in his mind already, not once but many times. He did not know Hardy, and Hardy did not know him. He would give Hardy the microscope, and Hardy would give him the money from the till, fifteen pounds at least, with luck, more.

There would be no questions asked; he would walk out of the shop as cool as a cucumber, and rich beyond his wildest dreams.

That was how he had planned it; only now, as the library clock ticked audibly towards a quarter to three, and the crucial moment approached inexorably, it did not seem quite so straightforward. Hardy might have a suspicious nature, and insist on knowing where Adam had got the microscope. Questions might, after all, be asked, and suddenly the proximity of Hardy's to the police station assumed a chilling significance. Then Adam was tempted, for reasons of cowardice rather than of repentance, to go straight to the bus station and take the first bus back to Garlet; he would be at Fox Farm in plenty of time to return the microscope to its place, before David came home from Angus's house. Then he could forget that any of today's events had ever taken place.

It was a strong temptation; not until he closed his eyes, shutting out everything, and conjured up in the darkness a vision of his dear Foxy, bright and intelligent and trusting to him for the gift of life, did Adam manage to brace himself. His resolution hardened grimly; he got up, handed over his book to be stamped, and stepped out with the parcel into the crowded street, a confusion of prams and a forest of umbrellas on the pavement, blanched by the brightness of shop windows behind. Walking half on the kerb and half in the gutter, Adam avoided the umbrellas and hurried up Kennet Street, before he had time to think any more.

Hardy's was the most dismal shop in a street of dismal shops. Its windows were furred with dust inside and out, its faded green paintwork splitting in long rents on the door and window frames. At first, Adam thought that it was closed, so dark it was, and in an instant of conflict did not know whether to be glad or sorry. When he peered through the panel of glass in the door, however, he saw that the interior of the shop was lit by one naked electric light bulb, hanging from the end of a twisted brown flex, much adorned with cobwebs. A pool of light fell poorly on the old-fashioned wooden counter, while further back in shadow loomed the shapes of old pieces of furniture, sideboards, wardrobes, sofas, looking disorientated and slightly sinister with no domestic order imposed on them. There was no sign of Hardy; only when Adam pushed open the door, setting in motion a horrible jangling bell attached to a wire spring, did he issue suddenly through a black doorway behind the counter, and approach, squinting at Adam through the gloom.

It was as if, all day long, Adam had been under an anaesthetic; but as the door swung shut behind him, and he faced the old man across the dirty, evil-smelling room, the truth broke upon him like a wave of sickness. He was a common thief, and worse than most, for he had stolen from his friends, and no reasoning or self-excuse on earth could alter that basic, hateful fact. He would have turned and run then, but for the thought of Foxy; he was a thief, and he loathed himself for it, but the spur to crime remained. Foxy must have food. Shuddering in his stomach, he approached the counter.

'Well, boy,' said Harold Hardy testily, drumming with impatient finger-nails on the varnished wood, and glaring at Adam through spectacles set over a bright red nose, 'what do you want? Out with it—I haven't got all day.'

It seemed an ungracious way to approach a customer, but the old shopkeeper was much troubled by boys.

Adam ran his tongue over his dry lips, swallowed hard, and said, 'I want to sell a microscope, please.'

'A microscope? And where did you get a microscope, eh?'
Adam did not answer, so the old man went on, impatiently,
'Come on, then—let me look at it. I haven't got all day.'

It was the second time he had said so; the remark was
habitual to him, although in fact he did have all day, every
day. Adam was his first customer since Thursday. Adam
undid the brown paper, and pushed the box towards him;
Mr. Hardy picked it up, and fumbled at the hook with cold,
rheumaticky hands. He took out the microscope, and
examined it in silence for a long moment, then he put it
down and looked hard at Adam through his thick spectacles.

'Where did you get this, laddie?' he asked again, not
accusingly, but with curiosity. As soon as he had realized
that Adam really was a customer, his normal tradesman's
good manners had reasserted themselves.

The lie came glibly enough from Adam's lips now: 'My
granny gave it to me for my birthday. I don't really want it,
so I thought I'd sell it, and buy something else with the
money.'

'Oh, yes. I see. And do your father and mother know?'

Adam was confused.

'My father's abroad,' he said. 'I—well, I don't think he'd
care.'

The old man nodded slowly, as he put the microscope
back in the box. Adam waited hopefully, expecting an offer;
all he wanted now was to get this business over, and escape
with the money into the street. Only when he saw the old
veined hands groping for the brown paper, and beginning to
wrap up the box again, did he realize, with shock, that his
mission had been a failure.

'I'm sorry,' said Mr. Hardy, 'but we can't do business. I
couldn't afford to give you a quarter of what this microscope is worth, and even if I could give you a decent price, I

wouldn't buy such a valuable piece without your parents' permission. It wouldn't be right. But if they do agree to your selling it, I suggest you take it to Kingsley and Potter, in Glasgow—179, Lanark Street West. They're honest folk —I used to deal with them in the old days—and they'll give you a fair offer.'

Then shame and self-hatred swamped Adam, making his knees tremble and his stomach contract in actual pain. He was a thief and a liar, while this old man was so honest that he would not do himself a good turn by buying something for less than it was worth.

Adam drew the parcel towards him, and said hoarsely, 'Well, thanks for looking at it, anyway. I'm sorry to have bothered you for nothing.'

'No bother,' said Mr. Hardy politely, and came round the end of the counter to open the door for Adam, and show him out, as if he were a favoured customer. 'Nasty afternoon,' added the old man. 'You'd best hurry home where it's warm.'

It was the politeness that hurt; now Adam felt that it was worse to be trusted than to be accused. He crept weakly down the pavement with only one clear thought in his mind; he would never steal anything again as long as he lived. But underneath the clear thought was dark knowledge; he had failed Foxy. Ninety-seven pence now stood between Foxy and the end of everything.

Afterwards, Adam could not remember very much about the journey back to Fox Farm; somehow, he found his way to the bus station, selected the right bus, and got off safely at Garlet Cross. In the rain, he stumbled down Rivergate to the school, unchained Richard's bicycle, and set off over the plain, pedalling grimly into the teeth of the wind. He was so tired that his mind turned mercifully blank; it was as if he needed all the energy he could muster to keep the bicycle on the road, and remember where he was going. The rain came stinging against his face, and soaked his trousers right through to his shins, but all the way, through the murky late afternoon, he kept his eyes fixed on the house at the croft, a dense black lump with rectangles of orange light cut out of its darkness. And into the emptiness that his mind had become came the thought of sausages, and eggs and fried bacon on blue plates, and the bright fire blazing in the kitchen range. Then through all his misery, Adam felt a tiny warm ray of pleasure, but he did not know that he felt it because he was coming home. The winter sun was sinking behind dirty grey tatters of cloud, a broken patch like tarnished pewter against a uniformly black pall, as he turned down the lane between sheltering hedges, thankful in his heart that a terrible afternoon was over.

Peculiarly, perhaps, the one thing which had not worried Adam was the possibility that the microscope would be quickly missed. This might have been because Richard was so insistent that David forgot its existence for months at a stretch; whatever the reason, Adam had confidently supposed that he was safe for some time to come. So, coming back from Millkennet, he had not rushed frantically to get the box back into the cupboard before David came back from Garlet; he assumed—and was still assuming as he entered the house with the box tucked under his coat—that all he had to do was wait, till David was watching television, or packing eggs, or in the bath, then slip unobtrusively into his room, and replace the microscope in the bottom of the cupboard. Thus he was completely unprepared, as he came through the hall and began to climb the stair on aching, exhausted legs, for the sound of David's voice raised angrily up above, and even then it was not until he had reached the landing half-way up, and was within earshot, that he realized the truth. Then horror passed over him like a cold wave of the sea.

For David was shouting, 'Of course you took it, so don't stand there looking innocent and trying to deny it. You were the one who wanted it last week, and who but you would have the cheek to steal it after I'd said "No"?'

Then there was Richard's voice, high and strained, but saying something very unexpected. 'I'm not denying it. But I didn't steal it. Borrowing's not stealing.'

First, Adam felt relief, then shame again.

'It's stealing when it's without permission,' said David. 'Now, go and fetch it.'

There was a horrible pause, while Adam stood petrified on the stair, then Richard said, 'I don't know where it is, exactly. I mean, it might be in one of two places. It may be in my room, but on the other hand, it may be in my desk at school. I don't exactly remember bringing it home yesterday.'

Then the row really got underway, with David stamping about, repeating, 'May be,' and 'Don't exactly remember,' and giving his opinion of borrowers and stealers in a very loud voice. Richard kept saying, 'Oh, stop it, Davie. Why do you have to make such a fuss?' Whereupon David ranted about the microscope's having cost thirty pounds, and ordered Richard to go at once and look for it in his room.

At this point Adam's paralysis left him. As a person who rarely lost his temper, he was rather contemptuous of those who did, and he could not help thinking, through all his fear, that David was making a complete fool of himself. Also, he knew that he had done enough things to be ashamed of for one day. Gone was the time when, hard and indifferent, he would have let Richard take the blame for anything and laughed to himself; now, with his whole life falling in ruins around him, he felt a burning desire to hear David Darke apologize to Richard. Steadily he mounted the last flight of steps, and walked towards David's room, but before he got there, the half-open door was thrown back and Richard came out, his face pale and young, with round, frightened eyes. The two stared at each other, and Adam realized that Richard knew everything.

'I was—' began Adam faintly, but Richard said, 'Sh!' violently, and pushed his foster-brother back towards the top of the stairs.

'Where is it?' he hissed, desperately.

'Here,' Adam replied, taking the parcel out from under his lapel. 'Don't worry, Richard. I'll go and—'

'Oh, shut up,' snapped Richard.

He snatched the parcel out of Adam's hands, tearing off the brown paper with wild fingers, and dropping it on the floor as he turned back quickly to David's room. He disappeared inside, and Adam heard him say perkily, 'There you are then. There's your precious microscope. I wish when you were looking through it, it could jump up and give you a black eye. In fact, I wish it was binoculars, so that it could jump up and give you two black eyes—Ouch, ow, stop it, Davie—he-e-elp!'

Adam expelled his breath through his mouth in a long sigh, and left them to it. He should have known how it would be; it was always the same with the Darkes. One minute they were ready to assault each other, the next they were rolling about laughing, the next they were the best of friends. But for him, it had been a very close shave, and why Richard should have covered up for him was puzzling. Adam went into his own room, changed his wet clothes, and waited for it to be time for tea. He hoped that Richard would not come in, and he did not; a few minutes later Adam heard him go downstairs with David, laughing and telling a story.

Adam was careful not to catch Richard's eye during tea; he dreaded the moment when they must be alone together. He did not talk either, but since he rarely wasted good eating time in conversation, his silence drew no comment. Richard was full of chat about his visit to Raven's Castle, and David about the white mice which he and Angus were breeding, and with which they expected to make their fortunes. They talked alternately; while one was eating, the other took over. If, by mismanagement, both happened to have their mouths full at the same time, Mr. Darke snatched the opportunity to report to his wife on the meeting of the Farmers' Union, telling her whom he had met, and who sent kind regards to her. It was a typical tea time at the Darkes'. Adam did not listen, but he grew warm and drowsy, so that the sharp edge of his humiliation was blunted; thus he was again completely unprepared when, almost at the end of the meal, Mrs. Darke suddenly clapped her hand across her mouth in dismay, then addressed him across the table.

'Oh, dear,' she said guiltily. 'How on earth could I forget such a thing? Adam, there's a letter for you from Australia—the post van brought it just after you'd gone. It's on the sideboard.'

Indeed, she did not know how she could have forgotten; she had been fretting about the letter all afternoon, as she baked pies and cakes and tended the oven, wishing heartily that she was wicked enough to tear it up, and put it on the fire, and say nothing about it to anyone. Sometimes it was very hard to do what you knew was right, when you suspected that the consequences might be terribly wrong. She looked at Adam anxiously, but the pale little face had its mask on, the features stiff, the blue eyes unrevealing. Wide awake in an instant, Adam got up in silence from the table, took the blue airmail letter from the sideboard, and went out of the room with it; the others listened to his feet mounting the stair, and the firm shutting of his bedroom door. They looked at one another uneasily.

'You don't suppose?' said David, and 'His father couldn't—after all this time?' said Mrs. Darke.

'No, he couldn't,' said Mr. Darke emphatically, his thick brows knotting in a frown. 'Whatever it's about, you can bet your life it isn't about *that*.'

As the father of sons, he was the Darke who felt most bitterly opposed to Andrew Hewitt as a person; if Adam's father had not been in Australia, it would have given kind, peace-loving Dick Darke great satisfaction to seek him out, and knock him to the ground. And he was right. It was not about *that*.

When Adam had heard the words, 'A letter for you from Australia,' his heart had almost stopped beating. He seemed to have been waiting so long, and so confidently, yet when he had taken in the fact that the letter had actually arrived, he had realized for the first time that deep down under his certainty there had been unacknowledged fear, that the letter would not reach its destination, that his father had left Targe Springs for another address, that—worst of all—Ruby would prevent his answering. But Hew had turned up trumps, Hew had not failed him. Then Adam felt a wild surge of joy and triumph, which ought to have issued forth in shouting and laughing and clapping of the hands, but because he had years of self-discipline behind him, years of keeping himself secret and not letting people know what he was thinking, he was able to get up in silence, stiffening his face, fetch the letter from the sideboard, and take it upstairs.

In the cramped little bedroom, he put on the light, sat down on the bottom bunk, and only then looked down at the printed address on the front of the blue envelope, with its stripes of red and a darker blue. 'ADAM HEWITT, c/o DARKE, FOX FARM, by GARLET . . .' he read, but—surely there was something wrong. Adam stared at the words, and for a long, stupid moment he could not think what it was, but then he knew; it was not his father's printing. He had seen that often enough on the Katoomba postcard, large, sprawling—manly, Adam would have called it. This printing was small, fussy, womanish—and with a sinking inside him, Adam knew whose it was. He flipped over the letter in his hands, and had his fear instantly confirmed. 'Sender's name and address: MRS. RUBY HEWITT, 6, NEW ROW, KENT FARM, TARGE SPRINGS . . .' Adam stared long and hard, then in a sudden, fierce movement he tore away the envelope and unfolded the single, flimsy sheet.

'Dear Adam,' he read. 'We got your letter on Friday and your dad has asked me to answer it as he is too busy on the farm. We don't know where you can have got the idea that your dad would want you to come to Australia, what can have put that idea in your head, it is impossible. We could not afford your fare, we have just moved to a new house and we have your little sisters to bring up and educate, but of course you do not know about them. You have three sisters, Robina $5\frac{1}{2}$, Sylvia 3, Shirley Ann 7 months. And we do not think you would like it here, you never liked living with us in Glasgow much now did you. And what is all this silly story about a fox I'd like to know, you would not be allowed to bring a dog into Australia let alone a fox. Not that we believe a word of it, and your dad says you are to stop romancing or you will get into trouble. We think it is a good idea if you behave yourself then the people you are staying with might want to adopt you. If you behave yourself. Your little sisters send love. From Mum (and Dad).'

Adam read the letter twice, then he sat for a long time, holding it in his hands. He knew that this was what he ought to have expected, perhaps even had expected in the darkest corner of his mind, where thoughts were not even acknowledged; in a dreadful moment of revelation which nearly tore him apart, he admitted to himself that his father was an unworthy recipient of the great love he had lavished upon him; that he always had been unworthy, even in those long-ago days when they had walked together on the beach, by the summer sea. It had nothing to do with Ruby; the fault was in Hew. Then something went hard in Adam; he did not cry, but calmly tore the letter into a hundred pieces, walked downstairs with them clenched in his hand, and scattered them on the rosy embers in the kitchen grate. They were so small that they blackened and shrivelled instantly, without flame, and fell down undramatically into the heart of the fire, taking with them all his aspirations, dreams and desires. Then he turned to David and Richard, who were watching him from the sink with solemn brown eyes, and said jauntily, 'What's on the telly tonight, then? I hope it's nothing about Australia, anyway.'

The flood of relief that broke over their faces should have been balm to him, if he had been capable of appreciating any comfort at all.

Impassively, Adam sat through a Western, a comedy show and a nature film, before the News began, and he and Richard were chased off to bed. More than anything, he would have liked to avoid the conversation with Richard which he knew must come when they were together in their room; despite his never sleeping in the house now, every night Adam had to go through the motions of eating his supper of cornflakes, washing, undressing, and getting into bed. Every Sunday, he and Richard exchanged bunks, knowing perfectly well that Adam would not be in his for more than three hours on any night. And although Adam knew that Richard would never, never ask him a question about the letter from Australia, he knew better than to suppose that the theft of the microscope would be treated with similar reticence.

Adam skipped washing, and hurried to get into bed while Richard was still downstairs; then, if things became too unpleasant, he could perhaps end the row by squirming down under the blankets and pulling the pillow over his head. When Richard appeared with the flask of soup under his jersey, Adam was sitting up in bed, very stiff, with a comic held up in front of his face. Richard put the flask on the chest of drawers, sat down heavily on Adam's feet, twitched away the comic, and said, 'You're a fool, Adam Hewitt. You're just a silly fool. What are you?'

'A silly fool,' repeated Adam dully.

And having got the other's attention, Richard launched into the remarks which had been choking him ever since afternoon.

'You must have known you'd be found out,' he scolded. 'Stealing from David of all people—you know how pernickety he is about his things. He knows where every blasted thing is, and he noticed the slide box had been moved the minute he opened the cupboard door. Suppose the microscope had really been gone—he'd have created the most awful fuss, and what then, eh?'

Adam did not answer this question out loud, but because he was feeling bitter, he gave a bitter answer inside his head.

'Then they'd have known I was a thief and a liar, and they wouldn't have wanted to have any more to do with me. So I'd have been sent back to old Hook at the double.'

But Richard went on, confounding him, 'You know, don't you? I'd have got a wee hiding for borrowing it, and a bigger one for losing it, as big as the one I got the night I set the pigs on fire, looking for my watch with a candle in the straw.'

They caught each other's eye, and a shared snort of heartless laughter cleared the air. It was the first time Adam had felt inclined to laugh at anything all day.

'Roast pork,' he said, and they snorted again. But—'Do you mean you wouldn't have told—even then?' he added, incredulously.

Richard turned up his eyes to the ceiling, and tutted in exasperation.

'Of course I wouldn't have told, fool,' he said, rolling the last word round his mouth, and savouring it with his tongue. 'If Dad had found out you'd actually pinched the damn thing, you wouldn't have been able to sit down for a fortnight. And suppose your lady Social Worker had got to hear of it—she might have thought we weren't to be trusted to keep you out of mischief, and taken you away from us. And you wouldn't have liked that, would you—separated from lovely me, and reunited with Mrs. Macaroni Pudding?'

In spite of the ache within him, Adam could not help laughing again.

'I couldn't get rid of it, anyway,' he told Richard. 'I took it to Hardy's, in Millkennet, but he wouldn't take it—said he couldn't afford to give me a decent price for it. He was a nice old man,' he added, remembering painfully the crumpled, threadbare waistcoat and cold, swollen hands.

Richard went up the ladder, delicately switching off the light with his big toe, although it was really Adam's turn. When they were both settled, with the covers pulled up round their chins, he said into the darkness, 'Adam.'

'Mn?'

'I've got some more money. Fifty pence in a postal order, from Granny. We'll go to the post office on Monday, and cash it.'

Adam did a quick calculation in his head; he was very good at money sums, nowadays. Ninety-seven, plus fifty. One pound forty-seven, and no hope of Australia any more. But he managed to thank Richard, warmly.

There was another silence, then Richard said, in the careful voice of a person who has been mustering his courage to say something which may not be well received, 'Adam, listen. I don't blame you for what you did—everybody does silly things when they're desperate. And you know you're welcome to the fifty pence, and my pocket money, and if I had anything else, you'd get that too. But surely you see—this can't go on. It isn't even April yet, and Foxy won't be able to fend for himself till June. I'll do whatever you decide—but I still think you should tell Dad.'

And this time Adam did not make a hurtful, angry retort; more than anything he would have liked to get up then, and go downstairs, in his pyjamas, to the sitting-room, and lean against the arm of Mr. Darke's chair, and tell him everything. Then he would ask Mrs. Darke if she would adopt him, so that he could be safe for ever with this family who seemed to love and want him, in spite of all his coldness and indifference to them in the past. But he could not, because, as he lay in the darkness, rolled up in a tight ball of pain and despair, he realized very clearly that nothing had changed. He could only purchase his own security by betraying Foxy; Mr. Darke was the same man who had shot the vixen, who would not—could not—have a fox at Fox Farm. Nor could he allow Adam to take a fox to a Council flat in a Glasgow street; everyone knew that fully grown foxes were smelly and destructive, and the neighbours would object.

Richard slept, and presently Adam got beyond the point where he could think at all. He lay listening to the clock on the stair, wiping away the minutes and the hours, waiting till it was safe to put on his clothes, and escape down through the storm-threshed wood to his bed in the tower. There Foxy would be waiting for him, trembling with joyous welcome; he would climb up into the rowing boat with Foxy, holding his pet in his arms, and where at last no one could hear him, he would cry himself to sleep.

In the News

For the next few days, Adam was overtaken by a great lassitude, as if his experiences on Saturday had been so terrible that his body and mind could not bear any more agitation for the moment, but must rest before he could begin to think again, and make plans. On Sunday, at lunch time, Mrs. Darke noticed his heavy eyes and whiter-than-usual pallor, and said to him kindly, 'What's the matter, dearie? You don't look well. Didn't you sleep very well last night?'

Adam admitted that he had slept very badly.

'Then I'll fill a hot-water bottle, and you can go up to bed till tea time. I hope you didn't catch a chill yesterday in all that rain.'

It was proof, Richard thought, of how miserable Adam was that he agreed to this, departing upstairs with the hot-water bottle under his arm, for Sunday afternoon was Foxy's special time, when the boys took him to play on the wide shingle beach down river from the croft, or into Hay's Field, a ten-acre meadow of tussocky grass, screened discreetly from the road by an overgrown beech hedge. There they ran over the winter grass, laughing and chasing and enjoying themselves, while Foxy circled round them, dancing and laughing in his own way, thrilled to be free in the fresh air, which to Richard had the finest smell in the world, sharp and salted by the nearness of the river estuary which was almost sea. The boys tired first; then they would sit in the warm lee of a dry stone wall, admiring Foxy as he made little forays into the grass after strange scents, following them and losing them, then coming bounding back to base, to sit on Adam's knee, or tickle Richard's face with his funny long tail. He had grown quite a bit since Adam had found him—and so he ought, Richard pointed out acidly, considering the high standard of feeding he enjoyed—but his tail showed no sign as yet of fluffing out into a beautiful Reynard's brush; it was as thin and ratty as ever.

Today, however, Richard had to leave Adam in bed, and go down to the tower alone. Between squalls, he took Foxy down along the shore, almost as far as Hutchinsneuk, where the great swing-bridge across the river was, and gave him an examination in obeying orders, '*Heel!*' '*Sit!*' '*Wait!*' '*Fetch it, boy!*' Foxy still had hazy notions about what was meant by fetching, but he could now pass all the other tests with flying colours, as Richard reported to Adam when he got home.

'You've made a really fine job of training that fox,' he said approvingly, sitting down on the foot of Adam's bed, 'far better than the man in the film. His fox wouldn't do a single thing it was told. I wonder if we should write to him, care of the BBC—maybe he could do with a few tips.'

'Maybe he just got hold of a stupid fox,' suggested Adam. 'Although I must admit that ours—' the word came from him quite naturally now '—ours is still pretty bad for chewing. He ate one of my socks the other night, and he's had a go at one of the blankets in the boat. But fortunately he hasn't touched the sleeping-bag—I don't think he likes the stuff it's sprayed with. It's got a funny smell.'

'I'm glad of that,' said Richard fervently.

The weather remained windy, and very dismal. On Monday and Tuesday the boys went to school as usual, cashed the postal order, and spent sixty-two pence of the remaining one pound forty-seven. They were economizing by giving Foxy a mixture of milk and water, so that a half pint bottle lasted for two days instead of one; the milk kept perfectly well in the icy atmosphere of the tower room, and, annoyingly in a way, Foxy did not seem to notice the difference.

'When the money runs out,' said Richard to Adam on Tuesday, as they came out of MacRae's with their little white polythene bag of minced beef, 'Foxy will jolly well have to eat scraps, whether he likes them or not.' It was said firmly, as if by being decisive, one could make it happen. 'He'll eat anything if he's hungry enough.'

It sounded a comforting theory, but Adam was not at all sure that Richard was right.

'Maybe he won't,' he replied worriedly. 'And if he won't, and he isn't fed, he'll get dangerous. Dogs do, even, and foxes are wilder than dogs.'

But he still felt ill and tired, so he shelved the problem till another day.

Then, on Wednesday, something happened which did nothing to help solve the problem, but created a diversion for the boys, and a sensation throughout the whole neighbourhood.

There was still no news of Major Robert Fauxe. Mr. Darke had learned this from Mrs. Fauxe herself, when he went up to Garlet Place to pay his quarterly rent; he had come back shaking his head over her gritty optimism, for the anniversary of the young man's disappearance had now passed, and Mr. Darke could not help feeling that the mother ought perhaps to be trying to face facts. David said it was the Weird, and nobody in the kitchen was inclined to disagree with him, except Adam, who was not in the mood for argument. One thing they were glad about, however, was that Mrs. Fauxe had the company of her daughter-in-law, the Major's wife, who had come to stay at Garlet Place till the end of April. Young Mrs. Fauxe came to Church every Sunday with old Mrs. Fauxe, to sit in the pew opposite the family memorial, and though Garlet church-goers were too polite to stare, they observed over their hymn books that she was a pretty lass, and seemed to get on well with 'the old one'. But the Fauxes were not people who took much part in village life; one remembered to feel sorry for them when one saw them, but that was so seldom that often days went by without the thought of them, or their Weird, ever crossing one's mind.

Then, overnight, they became famous, and for three days at least, no one in Garlet, Hutchinsneuk or the plain between thought much about anyone else.

It was Mr. Darke who brought the news home with him; he had been to the seedsman's in Millkennet in the afternoon, and had seen a poster for the *Northern Herald* outside a newsagent's in Kennet Street, screaming red, 'LOCAL FAMILY CURSE COMES TRUE'. Seized with foreboding, he had stopped the van, and gone in to buy a copy; drawing into a layby just out of the town to investigate, he had had his worst fears realized. Now he marched into the kitchen, his usually pleasant brown face red with indignation, and threw the folded paper down on the table with such violence that the three boys, who were packing eggs for the market, jumped with fright, as if they were being accused of something.

Mrs. Darke was preparing the evening meal.

'What's the matter, Dick?' she demanded, drawing her chip pan off the stove. She was aware that there was going to be a drama of some sort, and she did not want to add to it by having the kitchen go on fire half-way through. She approached the table, wiping her hands nervously on her apron.

'There,' said Mr. Darke, taking off his cap and jabbing at the newspaper with an angry finger. 'That's what's the matter. These poor women up at Garlet Place—haven't they had enough to suffer without some tomfool newspaper reporter getting hold of a story like that?'

'Like what?' cried Mrs. Darke, hastening to open up the newspaper. 'Oh, mercy—what's happened to them now?'

The boys left the eggs and crowded round her, trying to catch a glimpse of the offending article, which was spread, with shockingly familiar illustration, over the centre pages. With a peculiar feeling, they recognized a postcard-sized picture of the Victorian-Gothic façade of Garlet Place, with its pointed, churchy windows and absurd ornamental turrets, a glowering photograph of old Mrs. Fauxe, which looked as if it had been stolen from a police file, and another of Major Robert Fauxe and his bride on their wedding day. There were three headlines, one enormous, and the other two in smaller lettering:

THE MYSTERY OF
THE DISAPPEARING MAJOR
NEW LIGHT ON AN OLD CURSE
WHERE IS THE TREASURE NOW?

Underneath were several column inches of dense print, with a rectangular space in the centre, bearing the words, 'From the *Herald*'s Special Reporter'.

'Oh, glory,' said Mrs. Darke in dismay. 'Read it to me, David. I've left my specs upstairs.'

So David lifted the *Northern Herald* from the table, while the others kept their eyes fixed on him, groping with their bottoms for chairs, and read aloud the astonishing story which the Special Reporter had written.

'"In the year 1543, a Scottish nobleman, Lord Robert de Fauxe, known at Court as "The Fox", finding himself rather short of cash and rather fond of a luxurious life-style, helped himself to a Communion vessel, supposed to have been of great value, belonging to the Parish Church of Garlet-on-the-Hill, now a dormitory suburb of Millkennet. Unable to get his revenge in any other way, since the Fox owned the land on which the church was built, the Parish Priest, one Peter Alleyn, placed a Curse (known locally as the Weird) on the wayward lord. He declared that if the cup was not returned to the church, the family would lose both their titles and their lands, and the line would die out in the thirteenth generation. Since no one knew how Lord Robert had disposed of the stolen goods, this was not possible, and although his grandson replaced the cup with a better one, this act was not enough to remove the Weird, which has since come true. In 1745, the 5th Lord Fauxe and his three sons fought for the Stuart cause at Prestonpans and Culloden, and as a result were stripped of their titles and most of their estates. Only a year ago, Major Robert Fauxe, a 32-year-old officer in the Scots Guards, disappeared without trace from an Army team exploring the Terahucco, a remote tributary of the Amazon, in a region inhabited by savage tribes of Indians. Major Fauxe was thirteenth in line of descent from Lord Robert de Fauxe. He is survived by his wife, formerly Miss Marjorie Collingswood, who has no children.

'These astonishing facts lie behind a fascinating discovery lately made by Dr. M. Woolsey Prestwick, Guardian of the Butterhall Library, where many of Scotland's priceless historical documents and letters are stored. In the course of research for a book about the involvement of Scots mercenaries in the sixteenth century Spanish Wars in the Netherlands, Dr. Prestwick found a diary, running from June 1543 till May 1544, kept by Lord Robert de Fauxe while in self-imposed exile at Campveere. There was little of use to Dr. Prestwick, but the following sentences seemed to him of interest.

' "So I failled to bring that cup out with mee, for feare of mine enemies quho willed my downfall. I have therefoir sent orders to my lady to place it beneathe the butterie of my house at Garlett, and will recover the same when I come agane to that land."

'We know, however, that he did not again visit that land, since the date of that entry was 27th April 1544, and he died of smallpox at Ghent on 8th May in the same year.

'Dr. Woolsey Prestwick told the *Herald*, "Of course, we don't know for certain that Lady de Fauxe carried out her husband's instructions, or where exactly the buttery was, since the house which adjoined the present-day Fauxe Tower was demolished in 1840, but we do know that she died four days before her husband, and that news of his death did not reach Garlet till after her funeral. And since no cup has ever turned up between then and now which seems to fit the bill, it just could prove an exciting field of exploration for anyone interested in a piece of historical detection." '

'Could it, indeed?' interrupted Mr. Darke, with a furious growl. 'I'll give them historical detection if they dare to show their noses around here, I can tell you.'

Richard had never seen him look so fierce.

'Is there more, David?' asked Mrs. Darke.

David scanned the rest of the article quickly.

'Yes,' he said ruefully. 'It's all about Robert's father being killed at El Alamein, and about young Mrs. Fauxe— you don't want me to read all that, do you?'

'No, that's enough,' said his mother weakly. 'Dick, this is terrible. We'll be besieged.'

'Not if I have anything to do with it,' said Mr. Darke grimly. 'I'll put up notices. "Beware of the dog".'

Richard and Adam could not resist rolling their eyes at each other, but fortunately the others were too busy worrying to notice.

'To tell the truth,' Mr. Darke went on, 'I'm more concerned about these two women on their own up at Garlet Place. I think I'd better 'phone them, and offer to go up if they're being bothered. You know how stupid people can be.'

'Yes, do that, Dick,' said Mrs. Darke. 'Tell them the boys will come too, if they need them. Meanwhile, I suppose I'd better get on with the tea.'

The boys, although they felt sorry for the Fauxes, could not help applauding this decision.

Mrs. Darke returned to the chip pan, and the boys went to pack the last two trays of eggs, so that the table could be laid for tea. They could hear Mr. Darke in the hall, talking on the telephone, the usual one-sided conversation with long pauses punctuated with 'Mn,' and 'Ah'.

Presently he came back into the kitchen, looking relieved.

'Well, they're not as upset as I thought they'd be,' he announced thankfully. 'I spoke to young Mrs. Fauxe—the old one's in the bath. Apparently she's spent the whole afternoon composing letters to Dr. Woolsey Prestwick to tell him what she thinks of him, and to the *Herald* to ask where in thunder they got that photograph. They haven't had many visitors so far—the young one says they took the precaution of chaining up the main gate at lunch time, and when a few heads appeared over the wall in the afternoon, they let Harker and Tess out, and they soon disappeared again. I'd forgotten about the dogs. However, she says if they need any help she'll 'phone down for my sons—she thinks the red-headed one would be a good shot with a water-pistol.'

The red-headed son said he'd be a good shot with a gun too, but Mr. Darke said he didn't really think it would come to that.

'Do you suppose that cup is really buried down at the tower, Adam?' Richard asked later that night, as they went up to bed.

'No,' replied Adam flatly.

He had never been interested in the Weird, except as a story, and he did not believe in curses, although recently, as his capacity for caring had expanded, he had stopped laughing at Mrs. Fauxe's nose, and learned to be as sympathetic towards her as everyone else. Indeed, in one sense, he was more sympathetic, for he understood, as the Darkes could not, why she would not admit to herself that Robert was gone for ever. They thought she was being stubborn, and refusing to face facts, but Adam knew, from his own experience, that you do not allow yourself to believe that you have lost someone you love until the very last moment of proof. And, since Saturday, he had known how very terrible life becomes when once you do.

12 *A Night Fright, and What Happened Next Day*

Richard was very disappointed that he could not awaken, either in Adam or in David, enthusiasm for an excavation. Adam, when Richard hinted, as a lure, that the cup might be worth a lot of money, said sourly that the money would no doubt belong to the Fauxes, who had plenty already; if they wanted it, let them come down and have their own arms and legs scratched to ribbons in the brambles. Besides, he did not believe for one minute that the cup was there. Which sounded contradictory, but Richard could see that, in his anxiety about little Foxy, who was already on short rations of beef, Adam could not be bothered to think sensibly about anything else. David, on the other hand, did think that the cup might still be down about the tower, somewhere, but pointed out that it would be impossible to find it, simply because you would not know where to start looking.

'It isn't in the room where I keep the *Dragonfly*, we can't get upstairs because the door's bricked up, and to start looking outside would be like looking for half a needle in two haystacks,' he said. 'Think of it, Richie—we didn't even know there had once been another building beside the tower, did we? That's because every single trace of foundation is silted over with earth and mould, and covered with bracken and bramble. No. The only possible way of finding anything would be to go in with one of these metal-detectors—and we don't have one, nor are we likely to get one.'

'You could ask your Granny,' suggested Richard, heavily.

'Yes, I could, couldn't I?' mused David, who never recognized sarcasm when he heard it. 'Well—maybe in the summer, then. It's only sixty-three days till the O-levels, you see, and at the moment I have other things to think about.'

'The summer may be too late to save Major Fauxe,' said Richard tentatively.

'It's too late for that already. He's gone, poor fellow,' replied David sombrely.

But in any event, even if Richard had found a companion willing to scour the wood around Fox Tower, in the hope of finding the remains of the 'butterie' of wicked Lord Robert, the weather would have prevented any immediate expedition. For now it rained, and rained, and rained, melting the snow far away on the hills, filling the streams that filled the rivers, creating lakes in the fields and ponds by the roadside, until the whole earth seemed like a great sodden carpet that would never be dry again.

Fortunately, the rain also deterred the sightseers and treasure-hunters whom the Fauxes and the Darkes had expected and feared. The Fauxes kept their gates shut as a precaution, but reported no trouble; on Thursday the Darkes observed a few cars driving very slowly along the river road past Fox Farm, but none stopped, and all picked up speed further on towards Hutchinsneuk. The only incident which had to be dealt with occurred on Friday morning, when three young men in Wellingtons and waterproof cagoules came tramping down the farm road, carrying, in polythene wraps, an object which Mr. Darke later described to his more scientifically-minded sons as 'some sort of a vacuum-cleaner-like thing'.

'A metal-detector,' David said, and 'Fancy that,' replied his father.

Mr. Darke, who had seen the young men coming from the pigsty, cut through the yard and headed them off firmly at the yard gate.

'Eggs?' he asked. 'Potatoes? A winter cabbage? I'm afraid we haven't much else at the moment—it's too early in the year for plants.'

The young men halted, looking at him warily, yet half-sneeringly, trying to assess the situation. Then the one who was carrying the metal-detector decided to take the lead.

'Oh, we don't want to buy anything,' he said, with an attempt at a friendly tone. 'We just happen to be passing, and we thought we'd come down and have a look at that old tower place we could see from the road.'

Mr. Darke affected to be much astonished by this information.

'You choose poor weather for passing,' he remarked, 'if you don't want to buy potatoes, and you're not selling vacuum cleaners. Well, I'm sorry to disappoint you, lads, but this is private land, and you won't be having a look at the tower this day.'

The young men exchanged peevish looks, but Mr. Darke was a tall man and powerful, and they knew, and he knew, that he could have tossed all three of them over the gate.

However—'We'll see about that,' said one, defiantly.

Mr. Darke took one step towards him.

'I'll see about you, sonny, if you don't turn about,' he growled—with the result that the young men went up the road rather faster than they had come down.

The family much enjoyed this story, when it was told to them by the sitting-room fire in the evening; Richard, in particular, thought that he would have given a lot to see the intruders scampering up the lane with their tails between their legs.

That night, towards midnight, the rain stopped, and the cloud-curtains parted to admit three-quarters of a white moon. Adam was thankful; for the past four nights he had been unable to avoid being drenched between the shelter of the house and the shelter of the wood, and had had to go to bed in the tower damp and uncomfortable. Nothing and nobody, of course, could have persuaded him not to go; Richard had tried, but Adam replied that go he must, because Foxy expected him, and would spend the whole night crying behind the door, if Adam did not come. He did not tell Richard that he must also go because, deep within himself, he now believed that his life with Foxy was drawing to a close; even when he thought it, his heart seemed to dwindle to a tiny knot of pain in his chest, and his throat contracted so that he could not speak. He was so unhappy that he could keep nothing in his mind for more than a few moments at a time, so that, although he laughed with the others at Mr. Darke's story about the intruders—he liked Mr. Darke too well nowadays not to laugh at his jokes—by the time when he quietly closed the pantry door behind him, and set off in the glassy moonshine across the yard, he had already forgotten the matter completely.

Foxy always waited for Adam now in the little passage between the door and the stone room; he would bring with him a piece of the yellow ball, or a scrap of blanket, or a stick, and as soon as Adam pushed open the stiff, swollen door, the little creature would be on his feet, wagging his tail, quivering with joy, offering his gift in the little yellow pool of light shed by Adam's torch. Then Adam would bend down, and take the gift out of Foxy's soft mouth, fondling his ears and tripping over him as they went into the room, Foxy practically sitting on the toes of Adam's boots.

'Get off, you mad fox,' Adam would say, at which Foxy tried to climb up his trousers.

They would go up into the rowing boat together, and after Adam had drunk Richard's soup—Foxy did not care for soup at bedtime—and set the alarm clock for next morning, they would snuggle down in the cosy sleeping-bag and fall asleep. Adam was always tired out by anxiety and the lateness of the hour; normally he slept without turning till he was roused by the insistent shrilling of the alarm bell, and Foxy's nose pushing him gently in the face brought him up to start yet another anxious day.

Tonight, as usual, Adam switched off the torch, and was carried immediately into a deep, dreamless sleep. He did not know how long he slept, only that when he woke, it was not with the accustomed ringing in his left ear; instead, he seemed to have been startled into wakefulness by a noise which came from quite another level of consciousness, and because it had now stopped, he had no idea what it had been. It was still completely dark in the little stone chamber, where no moonbeams ever penetrated; poking up his head over the edge of the rowing boat, Adam could not distinguish the elongated rectangles which marked the window spaces of the room. Had he heard a noise, he wondered, or had he not? Foxy was awake too, alert, but not apparently alarmed; under his fingers Adam could feel the pointed ears thrusting upwards, pricking themselves, but Foxy did not attempt to come out of the sleeping-bag. He never cared for getting up in the morning, let alone in the middle of the night. Then a low hooting sounded overhead; they shared the tower with a family of barn owls who occupied the top floor, coming and going by doors of their own.

'It was only an owl,' Adam thought, yawning, and was preparing to go back to sleep when suddenly he heard again the noise which had really wakened him. It was not in the least like an owl-hoot, it was a metallic, clicking noise which seemed to come—automatically he turned his head to locate the spot—from just outside the largest of the arrow-slit windows, an opening some two feet by four inches, somewhat to the left of the door. And simultaneously, as if to verify Adam's guess, a wavering light crept through the window, up over the curved wall, picking out the Fauxe coat of arms, cup and tower and rampant fox, in the centre of the domed ceiling, and weaving off again across the damp-stained stone. Adam had never been in the least afraid in the tower before; aloneness and dark were nothing to him when he had Foxy at his side. Now, in contrast, he was absolutely terrified; even he, who believed in nothing he could not see, wondered if he were in the presence of ghosts. For a long moment he was so afraid of Sir Robert de Fauxe that human voices, when he heard them outside the window, came as a positive relief.

'Nothing there—better try this side then, Greg.'

'That's better—oh, damn these brambles. Nearly had my eye out. Hold the torch a bit higher, can't you?'

Immediately Adam realized the truth; it was not Sir Robert de Fauxe who was in quest of his cup, but the three young men who, unable to hunt treasure by day, had come back to try by night.

The voices roused Foxy; Adam felt his hackles rising, the tensing of his muscular little body, could hear the low, angry growl gathering in his throat. In an instant, his ragged barking would tear the silence to pieces.

'Quiet, Fox,' Adam whispered imperatively. 'Quiet, boy, do you hear?' And he put his hand over Foxy's cold muzzle, lightly holding his long jaws shut. Foxy obeyed, but his fur stood straight up along his spine, and rumbles of protest communicated themselves from his ribs to Adam's chest.

Adam was, as Richard had often observed, a very quick thinker; his head cleared by the disproving of ghosts, he realized two things at once. The first was that if he and Foxy gave themselves away, and called the men's attention to the fact that the tower was occupied by a boy and a small animal, they would have trouble. Adam had seen films in which children and animals fought criminals and won, but he was too much a realist to suppose that it would be so in actual life. He was not so much afraid for himself as for Foxy; brave little Foxy would fly at the men to protect his beloved Adam, and would be kicked, perhaps injured beyond relief. The second was that if he merely kept quiet and did nothing, the men with the metal-detector might find the cup—supposing that there was a cup—and get away with it, for he could not afford to raise the alarm and have them stopped. But Adam hesitated only a moment, then he knew what to do. In a crisis, all his natural coolness came to his aid; he would pay the men back, tit for tat, and at the same time have a little fun. So he kept his hand clamped over Foxy's snout for a while, and lay listening to the conversation. The historical detectives were not having a pleasant time.

'Over here, Kevin—no, look out—ouch, too late. It's full of water.'

'Yeah, you're right, and it's all gone down my wellies.'

'Okay then, Greg—give me the axe, and I'll just clear away some of this brushwood. Oh, for any sake, Norman. You've only got to hold the torch—hold it so's we can see what we're doing.'

'Ow-w-w-w!'

Adam enjoyed the 'ows' best. They were frequent, as the

men blundered about in the undergrowth, tripping over bramble runners and falling into the pools of water which had formed in every dip and hollow during so many days of rain. The clicking noises went on unceasingly until—

'Hang on a minute! Greg—Norman—there's something. . . . This is it, lads. Where's that spade?'

Then Adam sat up in the boat, took his hand from Foxy's mouth, and let everything go. He wailed and howled like a banshee, waking every echo in the little rounded room, while Foxy raised his voice in a crescendo of wild barking. Adam shone the torch round the walls, covering and uncovering the beam with his fingers, directing it towards the windows, then quickly hiding it again.

The panic outside was all he could have wished for.

'What the—'

'Oh, God help us, what is it?'

'Come on, boys, let's get out of this—'

There was a thudding of terrified feet past the door of the tower, diminishing as the treasure seekers reached the shelter of the trees, and made off in disarray through the wood; far off, Adam heard a car engine leap to life with a roar, and the tyres screaming off along the river road as if the car itself was fleeing from a ghost.

'Richard would have enjoyed that,' he said to Foxy.

Richard certainly enjoyed the experience at second-hand next morning, when he and Adam were feeding the hens together; they shared all their chores this way now, instead of doing them separately. For they who had never had anything to say to each other before, now could not find time for everything they wanted to say. At last they were real friends. Richard was full of open admiration for Adam's bravery and resourcefulness, and Adam basked in the other boy's warmth, thinking that nothing was ever quite so bad when Richard was by him.

'I think you were fantastic,' said Richard enthusiastically. 'You're so cool and cheeky, Adam. I'd have been scared out of my mind.'

'So was I, when I thought it was old Robert de Fauxe,' admitted Adam, throwing down handfuls of feed in front of the jerky, self-important brown hens. 'When I realized it was just people, I wasn't worried. You can always outwit people, if you're smart enough.'

Richard was not so blinded by affection that he did not think this a very conceited speech, but on the other hand, he had to admit that Adam had a very good success rate at outwitting people. Father and Mother, for instance, he thought with a shudder for trouble to come.

'Do you suppose they really had found anything interesting, with their detector?' he asked, as much to divert his own mind as to evoke an answer.

'Don't know,' said Adam, juggling with three eggs. 'It could have been just a tin can, you see. But never fear, my little man—after breakfast you and I are going to find out. It shouldn't be difficult to see where they finished up—they left so many tracks you'd think a herd of elephants had been watering at the river.'

Although he hadn't been interested when Richard first proposed it, he was now looking forward to the search. It surprised him, because he had never expected to look forward to anything again. The core of his misery remained hard and unbroken, but on the surface he felt much more like his usual, cocky self. It is not every night, after all, that one manages to control one's own irrational terror, and frighten three thieves out of their wits.

One might well have supposed that a herd of elephants had been watering at the river. Later in the morning, when Richard and Foxy joined Adam in surveying the area round the tower, they were shocked that so much havoc had been caused by three men; the grass was laid flat, the bracken ground into a sea of black river mud. Foxy ran to and fro, snuffling with his sensitive nose, while the boys, less expert at picking up scents, investigated the footprints which seemed to go in every direction, many now up to the brim with water, like shoe-shaped pools. But Adam had been too optimistic; it was impossible to tell where the intruders had ended up.

It was a pity, as Richard said, that they had had the sense to hold on to their equipment when they ran; a dropped torch, or a spade, would have been a very useful clue to the whereabouts of the object which the metal-detector had detected. What they did find—although not until Richard had tripped over it, and fallen into the brambles with an anguished squawk—was a block of grey stone; further investigation, with the aid of the shovel which Richard kept in the tower 'for cleaning up after your fox, Adam Hewitt', showed that this was part of a submerged wall, the foundation, evidently, of the house which Dr. Woolsey Prestwick said had once adjoined Fox Tower.

The boys explored the wall for some time, scraping away the mud and bracken which clung to the stone, tracing the line along to a corner of the building, and a little distance down the adjacent side. They might have gone on until they had uncovered the whole perimeter of the house, but as things turned out, that had to wait till summer came, because Adam suddenly noticed that Foxy had disappeared.

'Blast,' he said, putting down his shovel. 'Where's he gone

to? Foxy! Hey there, where are you? Come on, Fox, come on, old boy!'

But Foxy did not come.

Richard joined in, 'Foxy! Here, Fo-o-oxy!'

But Foxy did not come. The boys looked at each other, wary of showing their anxiety too clearly.

'He can't be far,' Richard said.

'No,' said Adam, trying to be calm, but sounding uncertain.

For into both their minds came the thought which they never put into words but which was never far away, that Foxy was of the wild, and at any moment might follow his instinct and be gone.

Adam said, 'Richard, I can't lose him. Not this way. Never to know—' but Richard, steadier because he was not quite so deeply involved, said, 'Don't panic, Adam. He was here a minute ago. I expect he's gone down a rabbit hole— this wood is riddled with them. We'll keep calling, and see if we can clear away some of this bracken, and find an opening.'

Richard was almost right, but not quite. While the boys worked, Foxy had been very busy too, for a while, intoxicated by the scents of strange creatures, but disappointed because none of the fascinating trails he discovered led him to any interesting quarry. He had sniffed and snuffed and run anxiously round, trying to help, and he had tried to explain to Adam and Richard what a hard time he was having, and how they ought to stop shovelling earth, and talking, and commiserate with him. But they would not, and when he pushed his nose between Richard's knees, or slapped Adam's hands gently with his tail, they said, 'Get off, Fox—we're busy,' which was not at all the treatment Foxy was used to. So when he found what he thought was a large, inviting rabbit hole, he went down it in a huff, and instantly wished he hadn't, when he found himself in an extremely dark and unwelcoming passage below. And it got even darker.

Sniffing about among a surprising pile of objects made of metal and wood, and pieces of broken delf Foxy stuck his long nose into the open end of a cylindrical object, and couldn't get it out again. It seemed to cling to his face, and no matter how he banged about in the darkness, frantically trying to dislodge it, the thing stayed put, wedged over his nose so that he could scarcely breathe, let alone cry aloud for Adam to come and help him, as he wanted to do. Then in anguish he began to run up and down the hateful place trying to find a way out; it was by accident, purely, that he emerged into the world through the hole he had gone down, just as Adam and Richard, white-faced and almost in tears, clawed away the bracken and bramble which covered it.

Neither of the boys felt inclined to laugh, although poor Foxy looked comical enough, with his face masked by a metal pot with two great curly handles, like ears sticking out from his head; Adam gently prised off the offending object, then without looking at it, hurled it furiously away from him into the brambles. But Richard marked where it fell, and while Adam hugged Foxy, and shed tears of relief on to his furry throat, he plunged after it through the wet bracken, his heart suddenly leaping with excitement.

13   *Foxy*

'It's not at all what I expected,' said Richard later, when they had comforted Foxy, and taken him into the tower to be brushed and cleaned up with an old towel. 'I'm a bit disappointed, really—I thought it would be gold, or silver, you know, and perhaps covered with jewels—not a horrid, dingy old thing like this.'

The cup lay between the two boys on the floor, a dented, blackened container, about seven inches high, with a wide mouth and sides which sloped in straight to a smaller base. It had curly handles, and a raised pattern of leaves around its lip, but there was not much else to be said except that it was filthy, both inside and out.

Adam picked it up, running his fingers over the tarnished surface, and said thoughtfully, 'It's impossible to tell what it might have been like, once—you can't even tell what it's made of, except that it's metal of some sort. But—' glancing up '—it isn't at all like the cup in the coat-of-arms. That's shaped like a wine glass, but this is more like a vase, isn't it?'

'Yes,' said Richard dubiously; then, cheering up, 'But of course we don't know what Communion cups were like in fifteen-something, do we?'

'No.'

'Adam—you do think this is it, don't you?'

'Oh, yes, sure to be,' said Adam easily, wanting to please Richard. For himself, he did not care whether it was, or whether it was not.

Richard felt reassured. Ever since he had seen poor Foxy come blundering out of the hole with the cup wedged over his nose, he had been willing himself to believe that there was no doubt in the matter; now he was right on the brink of succeeding.

'What fun it will be, showing it to Mother and Dad and David at lunch time,' he said gloatingly. 'Won't they be surprised?'

But in the silence which followed his question he realized that for some reason they would not be showing the cup to the others at lunch time. 'Well, why not?' he asked flatly.

Adam, who was sitting on Foxy's bed, with the cup in his hands and Foxy stretched out over his feet, looked miserably at Richard.

'I'm always spoiling things for you,' he said, his pale red eyebrows meeting in a frown. 'But—well, look at it this way. If we show the cup now, we have to explain how we found it, and even if we do leave out the bit about Foxy, it's most likely that David and your Dad will want to come down here in the afternoon to see the place, and—'

'And Foxy will bark when he hears strangers, and give himself away,' finished Richard. 'Yes, of course. I hadn't thought of that. Say no more.'

He felt regretful, yet when he reminded himself of the many strands of falsehood and half-truth that would have to be woven into a credible explanation, he knew that it was far better to keep silence. Only—'What about Major Fauxe?' he could not keep from asking.

Richard had seen Major Fauxe only once in all his life, three years before, on the day when he was married in Garlet Church, yet the thought of that doomed young man lost in the forests of the Amazon seemed to haunt him, as if he were a friend. His desire that Major Fauxe should come safely home was second only to his desire that Adam should be able to keep Foxy, and stay on with the Darkes until they

were both grown up. But because it was second, he accepted
Adam's plea.

'Honestly, Richard, it can't make any difference to Major
Fauxe. He's been missing a year. If he's dead, he's dead. But
Foxy's still alive. Please?'

Richard winced inwardly at the desperation in the boy's
voice, and once again he was overwhelmed by a dreadful
sense of the hopelessness of everything. There was only.
meat and milk left for three more days.

'Adam, tell Dad,' he urged. 'Tell him now.'

But Adam shook his head.

'I'll think of something,' he said.

So they wrapped up the cup in a couple of Mr. MacRae's
polythene bags, and hid it in the bottom of the boat, under
the duckboard. Then they fed Foxy, climbed down on to
the shore to wash the mud from their boots in the river, and
went slowly home to lunch. And that would have been that,
for a few days more, had not something happened in the
meantime which forced Adam into the very course of action
which he had tried so hard to avoid.

A few hundred yards up river from Fox Farm there was a
place where the boys never went; it was the junction of the
great, ship-bearing river and one of its tributaries, a stream
called the Lintie Burn. The Lintie rose far away in the hills,
and came weaving down through fields and woods, chuckling busily over stones, and forming dark still pools under
trees for trout to lie in, until at last it came to Garlet Plain,
and widened out to meet the river on its way to the sea.

Up at its source, and for most of its journey, it was a
pleasant stream enough, living up to its lightsome name as it
pattered through green meadows, under little stone bridges,
reflecting sun and leaves in its brightly moving water. But as

it drew near the end, its nature seemed to change; it deepened suddenly, and flowed out dark and smooth and silent between steep banks of sedge-crowned mud. The boys were forbidden to go down to its mouth alone, for the black mud banks were treacherous, and the currents strong; they were not, however, tempted to disobey, because it was one of those sinister, desolate places which one avoids by instinct. David loathed the high singing of the wind through the reeds, and Richard hated the delicate shivering of the water where it merged into the great river, as if it were suddenly chilled by a breathing over its surface.

Sometimes, in rainy seasons, the water in the Lintie Burn rose so high that it overflowed its banks, flooding the meadows and causing much damage to the carpets at Fourwells Farm, and the low-lying cottages on the Garlet Road. Then Mrs. Darke thanked Heaven loudly and often that the Fox Farm buildings stood on a little rise; it had been known for the road and the fields to be under nine inches of water, and the house standing high and dry.

Now there was danger of flooding again; the heavy rains of recent weeks had filled all the streams of the plain to the brim; they were hurrying down feverishly between torn, straining banks, as if they had a race to win, churning and chattering and eager to pitch themselves into the great grey river which had room for them all. It had been obvious for days that the Lintie was carrying more water than its banks could cope with; up at the bridge on the Garlet Road, the restless fawn flood was within six inches of the keystone, and the peaceful nights of Fox Farm were disturbed by its roaring. Further down, at its mouth, it was as silent as ever, but there too its level had risen to the top of the banks, and where previously it had been perfectly still, now it was on the move, stirring and seething like a pot coming to the boil.

It rained again all day on Sunday, and on Monday after-noon, when yet more puffy black clouds were forming ranks beyond the river, Mr. Darke said to his wife, 'I'm going up to have a look at the Lintie, Mary. If it's likely to flood—and I'm pretty sure it is—I'll move the straw out of the stable into the loft, just in case the water comes a bit further up than usual. I can't afford to take chances.'

So he put on his waders and set off, ploughing through sinking turf and across brimming ditches; it took so long to get to the river that he decided to come back by the road, and so met Adam and Richard coming home from school on the bicycle, Adam pedalling while Richard sat on the saddle-bag behind. The boys got off, and walked the rest of the way with him. Clouds blotted out the watery sun, and night fell in the middle of the afternoon.

'There's going to be a flood,' Mr. Darke told them.

'I thought so, when I saw the water at the bridge,' said Richard. 'But—are you positive, Dad?'

'If we have one more night of rain,' said Mr. Darke, glancing up at the navy blue sky, 'you'll be swimming to school in the morning.'

Adam thought this would be fun, and laughed a lot, picturing Puss's reaction when he arrived in his trunks, shedding water all over the classroom floor. But Richard looked very grave; as soon as they got to the house, he called Adam into the pantry, and shut the door.

'What's the matter?' asked Adam, suddenly aware of Richard's scared face. 'Foxy—'

Whenever he sensed trouble, his thoughts flew to Foxy.

'Yes, Foxy,' said Richard. 'Now listen, Adam—this is serious. We've got to get Foxy out of the tower tonight, and you can forget about sleeping there. You've never been here when there's been a bad flood, but that tower is at the bottom of a hollow, and every time the Lintie overflows, it's under three feet of water in no time. Dad says that's why people stopped living in it. If we leave Foxy there any longer, he's going to be drowned.'

As this terrible truth sank into his mind, Adam felt his legs buckling under him, and he sat down heavily on a convenient stool.

'What are we going to do?' he asked thickly. 'I can't think.'

'You must,' said Richard. 'He belongs to you, and what you say goes. I'll back you up—you know that—but you know what I think too, Adam.'

Adam stared at him, his white face stiffening into a peculiar mask of greyish-green.

'Not yet,' he whispered. 'I've got to have time.'

'There isn't time. You'll have to decide now.'

Adam sat very still on the stool for a long moment, then in a convulsive movement he rose, and bolted out of the room. Richard could see him from the little pantry window, running across the yard like a blind person, stumbling instinctively towards the dark mouth of the wood. He sighed, and looked at his watch. Ten to four. He would give Adam twenty minutes, then he would go after him; by that time he would be in need of company, and support.

Adam blundered down between the dark trees, seeing only vaguely through the distorted glass of his tears. For the most part, he avoided the roots and creepers which spread across his path, ready to trip him up, and presently he arrived at the tower, pushing blindly at the door with fingers scarcely aware of what they touched. Foxy was waiting for him in the passage, for it was time for his after-school run along the shore, but he did not greet Adam with his usual vociferous delight. It was as if he too sensed something wrong in the little secret world of which he was the hub, for he ran up to Adam silently, and when the boy squatted down to lift him, squirmed hastily into the space between Adam's jerkin and jersey, which seemed to him the safest place in the world. Adam carried him into the stone room, and sat down on the floor with his back against the wall, hugging Foxy to him in the most terrible, lonely moment he had ever known, even in a life already too full of such moments. For in the past, other people had betrayed him, but now, he was to be the betrayer. Too unhappy even to cry properly, he sat in the darkness with Foxy, while his pain communicated itself to the little animal, who whimpered softly as he rubbed himself against Adam's chest, and pushed his nose into the hollow between Adam's shoulder and his neck.

For a while, Adam could not form thoughts into words. He only knew that he had come to the end of the way he had chosen. His plan of a new life in Australia had come to nothing, he had no money left, and now, in a cruel turn of fortune, it seemed that even Nature was against him. There was nowhere else to hide Foxy on the croft; he and Richard had come to that conclusion on the day when he had found Foxy at the notice-board tree. Now Adam was left with two bleak choices; he could betray Foxy, or he could let him be drowned, that night, when the flood came across the fields.

'It has to be this way, Fox,' he said. 'I've done my best, I have, honestly. You know that, don't you?'

Foxy seemed to indicate that he knew Adam had done his best.

'We'll have to hope that things will work out, then—we'll have to trust Mr. Darke. He'll know what to do, I think. Are you listening, Foxy?'

Foxy was listening. He did not know what Adam was talking about, only that Adam needed comforting. So he comforted him as best he could.

Richard arrived. He came and sat down beside Adam on the floor, and tickled Foxy's ears, because he was too shy to touch Adam. Then he said, 'What have you decided?'

Now Adam's voice came high and clear again. 'To take Foxy to your Dad,' he said. 'I have to—I've thought of everything else, and nothing works. Will you help me?'

'Yes. What do you want me to do?'

'Go up to the house ahead of me. I don't want to walk in with Foxy, and start trying to explain. Tell your Dad I've been keeping a fox in the tower—he won't blame you, for it was my idea from the first. Then I'll bring Foxy up, and we'll see what happens. Will you, Richard?'

'Sure,' said Richard.

He was not at all convinced that he would not be blamed, and he fully expected trouble ahead, but he was relieved that at last Adam had taken a decision, and that all the deception and danger were coming to an end. He got to his feet, and said as cheerfully as he could, 'It'll be all right, Adam, so don't worry. I'll go and tell Dad now.'

But before he went, he remembered to jump up on to the end of the trestle table which held up the boat, and take out the hidden cup, in its shroud of white polythene.

Adam waited for ten minutes before he rose and followed Richard up through the wood, but it seemed like hours and hours. And still, when he eventually went out among the evening trees, with the roaring of the waters drumming in his ears, it seemed to him that time was suspended, that it took for ever to walk the few hundred yards which separated the secret places where he had been with Foxy from the everyday world where he lived with the Darkes. He held

Foxy close against him, so that he could feel the throb of the animal's heart beating against his own, and he was in pain for Foxy, yet as he came to the mouth of the wood, and began to cross the yard in the gathering darkness, he was at peace, like a person coming to the end of a much longer journey. For now Adam had come to the most important decision he would ever make in all his life. Whatever Mr. Darke decided about Foxy, he, Adam, was going to stay with the Darkes; at last he accepted that if Mr. Darke said that he and Foxy must part, it was because, in human terms, there was no other way out. But Adam knew that Mr. Darke would not inflict such pain on a son, if a way could possibly be found to let him and his pet stay together. He would trust Mr. Darke, and it would be easier because he had already trusted Richard, who had never let him down. Yet there was a great sob in his throat as he pushed open the kitchen door, and stepped from the dim, timeless world into the humdrum shine of the electric light.

The Darkes were grouped around the kitchen fire, looking like people on a stage, frozen into one position as the curtain rose. Mr. and Mrs. Darke were sitting in the armchairs on either side of the hearth, he with his huge feet in grey woollen socks, for he had been in the act of removing his boots when Richard entered, she in her flowery apron, ready to start cooking the evening meal. David was squatting on the hearth rug with his back to the blaze, while Anne, who had just come home for her day off, was perched on the arm of her father's chair, still wearing her nurse's cap and navy blue coat, with a blue and white striped dress underneath. Richard was standing in front of them; when Adam came in, he left the group by the fire, and realigned himself at his foster-brother's side. No one said anything; the brown-eyed Darkes looked at Adam, and at the little foxy head peeping out interestedly from the opening of his jerkin, and were really too astonished to say anything at all. Richard's story had seemed to them a pack of improbable nonsense, yet here was the boy, with some kind of animal clutched in his arms.

It was Foxy who first decided that it was time for somebody to make a move. Drawn by the unaccustomed warmth he slipped out of Adam's arms, leaped lightly down and trotted confidently across the brown linoleum to the fire. He nudged David out of the way with his nose and his bottom, and having cleared the best position on the rug, lay down, curled up, and closed his eyes. The tension was broken; the Darkes looked at Adam and Richard, looked at Foxy, looked at each other, and burst out laughing. Bewildered, Adam and Richard only looked at each other.

'I don't understand,' Adam said. 'It doesn't seem funny to me.'

There was something in his voice which quelled the laughter. Mrs. Darke looked at him closely, and Mr. Darke sobered up, shaking his head warningly at David and Anne.

'Come you here, Adam,' he said kindly.

Adam walked across the floor towards him. He kept his eyes fixed on Mr. Darke's weatherbeaten face, because in this unreal situation it was easier to look at one thing at a time. He could not fathom why it was that Mr. Darke still looked amused, but it was better than anger, he supposed. The amusement should have been a hint, but it was not; he was so sure of all his own surmises about Foxy that he was completely unprepared for Mr. Darke's question.

'Adam, what on earth made you think that wee beast was a fox?'

Adam's head reeled; his throat tightened, and he could not have spoken, even if he had known what to say. Mr.

Darke put his arm round him, and he leaned against Mr.
Darke's shoulder until he found a small voice, and said, 'We
found him on the day after you—had to shoot the vixen.
We—that is, I—thought he looked like a little fox, and I
wanted to save him. He was so small and frightened. I knew
you couldn't have a fox about the croft, but I wanted him to
have a chance to live. Richard helped me, but it was all my
idea.'

Mr. and Mrs. Darke exchanged looks, and Mrs. Darke
said, 'Of course, that's right enough, Dick. It was just about
that time they found two pups on the road up at
Fourwells—I remember Mrs. Hopkins telling me about it at
the W.R.I. They thought someone had brought them along
in a car, and abandoned them at the farm gate.'

'Who would do such a thing?' exclaimed Richard indignantly.

'I don't know, love. There are some nasty folk in the world.'

Feeling a bright trickle of hope seeping through the black
wall of his despair, Adam hardly dared to ask. 'Then he
really isn't a fox?' he said hoarsely.

'No, he's not a fox. I wouldn't have shot the vixen if there
had been any chance she'd have cubs, Adam. She'd still
have had to go, later, and probably they would, too, but I'd
have given them a clean death, not left them to die slowly of
starvation. But I knew it was too early in the year for a
litter—April's the time, or late March at the very earliest.
No—your fox is a dog, of some kind, although just what
kind is not so easy to say.'

He looked down at Foxy, who was certainly not recogniz-
able as any particular breed of dog, and scratched his head
in a puzzled way.

'A bit of a corgi at the head, maybe,' said David, trying
to be helpful and starting to laugh again.

'And a bit of a whippet in the middle,' suggested Anne, grinning.

'And a bit of a rat at the tail,' David could not resist adding, as he went off into fits of laughter which Richard could not help joining. But he was laughing mostly at himself, as he recalled all the things which should have warned him that Foxy was no fox. Whoever heard of a fox with a stringy tail, who wore a collar and walked at heel, and was so faithful and loving and anxious to please? He was as unlike the film-fox as—well, as dog from fox, actually. So Richard laughed towards Adam, expecting him to share the joke, which was against them both. But Adam watched him with hurt, angry eyes.

It was Mrs. Darke who got the situation under control. She got up and said, 'Adam, come away into the sitting-room with Dad and me. We've got things to talk about. We'll leave these daft ones to make the tea—that'll calm them down. Take off your coat, Anne, if you're thinking of staying—there's steak in the 'fridge, and the potatoes are ready to put on.'

Adam never told anyone what he said to Mr. and Mrs. Darke that night, in the privacy of the sitting-room, nor what they said to him, yet somehow the very happy conclusion to their conversation seemed to escape from the room before they opened the door. For when Adam came out, Anne and David were waiting in the hall to thump him cheerfully on the back, and shake him by the hand, and when he went upstairs to hang up his jerkin, with Foxy prancing merrily at his heels, he met Richard coming out of their room, carrying the suitcase which had contained the sugar bag, and the postcard of *Sunset over Katoomba*.

'I put your watch on the chest of drawers,' he announced,

'and I'm taking this suitcase up to the attic. You won't be needing it again in a hurry, I suppose.'

Oddly, perhaps, it was Richard who expressed least delight to Adam directly, yet he was so happy that when, later, he produced the 'Communion' cup, and passed it around the table amid more gales of incredulous laughter, and was informed that it wasn't much better than an old tin can, he hardly minded at all. Only for Major Fauxe, of course, and that fear was wiped away for ever at nine o'clock that same night, when young Mrs. Fauxe telephoned to tell them that she had had a telegram from Chiquinquira, saying that Robert was safe and well, and would be flying home at the end of the week.

14   *Fox Farm*

That night, Adam slept soundly in his own bed, with Foxy stretched out serenely at his feet. Never again in all his life would he know such a moment of perfect relief as when he had said breathlessly to Mr. Darke, 'Am I allowed to keep him, please?' and the father had replied in his slow, easy way, 'Of course you're allowed to keep him. I was just saying to Mother the other day that it would be nice to have a dog around the place again, but the lads never seemed to want another one after Shep was run over on the road. You can keep him, and welcome.' Very little had been said about Adam's sleeping out in the tower, and the various other deceptions the boys had practised; relief was in the air, and as Mrs. Darke said, there was little point in making a fuss about things that could never be changed now, anyway.

Foxy, for his part, seemed very pleased with all the civilized arrangements of the house, which he perhaps felt were in accord with his new status as a dog; he had staked out his claim to the central position on the kitchen rug, and had dined on a ham bone and some leftover stew, listening wisely while Mrs. Darke explained that since she couldn't afford to buy him minced beef every day, he would have to learn to like what was available. Foxy had been very friendly towards Mrs. Darke; indeed, he was very friendly towards all his new acquaintance, but he left no one in doubt as to where his heart was first given.

When the boys went up to bed, the rain was streaming down over the fields and the wood; behind its quiet, unhurried plashing they could hear the angry tumult of the Lintie Burn, straining its banks to breaking point as it hurtled towards the river. They fell asleep with flood noises in their ears, but woke in the morning to silence. At three o'clock the banks had suddenly yielded, and the pent water had dispersed itself, covering the Fourwells fields, the Garlet Road and the meadows alongside the river with a film of shimmering grey. Fox Farm was on an island; when they got up, Adam and Richard could see that the wood too was under water, for as the sun rose in a washed blue sky, it made shining pink reflections around the bases of the trees.

'We won't be able to go down to the tower today,' said Richard, as he dragged his jersey over his rumpled brown head.

'What would we be wanting to go down to the tower for?' asked Adam happily. 'No one lives there any more.'

They were not able to go to school either. Before breakfast, Father waded out to test the depth of the water at the road end, and came back to tell the boys that it was too deep to risk taking the van out. Mrs. Darke said she would 'phone the schools, and say that the boys would come tomorrow, if the flood had gone down.

'A holiday from Puss,' said Adam, with satisfaction.

'A holiday for Puss, I'd say,' muttered David, whereupon a little fight broke out, with Foxy joining in eagerly on all sides.

So the boys had a day of unexpected leisure, which they spent teaching Foxy to field a cricket ball in the morning, and to jump through a hoop in the afternoon. He was not very good at either of these things, but he willingly demonstrated for David how well he could sit, and wait, and come to heel.

'Did it never occur to you duffers,' asked David curiously, when they were resting from cricket on the back doorstep, 'that you couldn't teach a fox to come to heel? Remember that film we saw on television, Richard? The fox was untrainable.'

'I know that. But we thought ours was a specially intelligent fox,' Richard explained.

'Well, he's not a specially intelligent dog,' said David rudely. 'He's eating your jersey.'

'He is a specially intelligent dog,' said Adam complacently, as Richard howled, and snatched his jersey away. 'He always eats Richard's things, but he never touches mine. I can't think of anything more intelligent than that, really.'

A week passed, and the floods receded from the fields, until all that remained was a scatter of ponds and puddles, like lakes in microcosm among the grass. An obliging wind blew up to help dry out the plain, the Lintie Burn resumed its accustomed course, and life at Fox Farm went on as usual, except that Mr. and Mrs. Darke had acquired a third son, and there was a little dog with a long thin tail lying on the rug by the kitchen fire. It was almost spring, and in the sunshine, and the sudden greening of the hawthorn hedges, there was promise of summer to come. David said that he was going to build a canoe in the woodwork class at school, as soon as the exams were over, so Richard and Adam could have the *Dragonfly*; almost unable to believe their good luck, the two made a happy expedition to Millkennet to buy paint, so that they could prepare their craft for launching at the beginning of May. They decided to remove the word *Dragonfly*, and rename the boat the *Foxy*.

'Do you know, I believe they've all forgotten what's going to happen in September,' said Mrs. Darke to her husband, as she watched Adam and Richard collecting paint brushes and turpentine and old shirts, and running off down through the wood, with Foxy bouncing at their heels.

Mr. Darke put on his tweed jacket, and took down an envelope from the chimney piece. 'Let them enjoy this summer while they can—next year it will all be very different. However—' he sighed '—what will be, will be, and at least they'll have each other. I'm just going up to Garlet Place with this letter, Mary. It's my notice to Mrs. Fauxe that we're quitting at the end of the summer. And where's that cup thing the boys found? I thought I'd take that, too—it might help to change the subject if the old lady's inclined to argue.'

Mrs. Fauxe did not argue, but neither did she open the letter. She took it quietly from Mr. Darke in the gloomy drawing-room, with gold-flocked wallpaper and ecclesiastical windows, and laid it on her desk. Then she turned sharply, and said in her sudden way, 'You know my son is home?'

Mr. Darke said he did, and was glad for her, and tried not to feel hurt because she so quickly turned the conversation away from his affairs to her own. It was natural enough, no doubt.

'Ah well, we'll see, we'll see,' said Mrs. Fauxe enigmatically, and when she had smiled over the cup, and asked what Richard had to say about the Weird now, she got up, and Mr. Darke got up, and soon was shown out again into the sunshine. He drove slowly down the drive, feeling that it had been an unsatisfactory interview; surely, after all these years, Mrs. Fauxe might at least have said that she would be sorry to see him go.

The following afternoon, however, when the whole family happened to be gathered in the kitchen at Fox Farm, Mrs. Fauxe's Jaguar careered unexpectedly into the yard, and screeched to a halt outside the back door. Mrs. Fauxe's untidy, felt-hatted head could be seen emerging from the driver's side, but when Mrs. Darke hurried to open the door—Mrs. Fauxe's arrivals were always too spectacular to require a discreet knock to announce them—she saw that the old lady was not alone. Coming round from the other side of the car was a tall man with fair hair and a large nose, too like Mrs. Fauxe to need any introduction; it was her son, Robert.

They came into the kitchen, and sat down on the chairs vacated for them; Mrs. Fauxe said, 'Yes, thank you,' to Mrs. Darke's suggestion of a cup of tea, and Mrs. Darke and Anne began to move between the sideboard and the table, laying out cups and saucers, cutting some slices of currant cake. The boys sat where they could watch Major Fauxe without seeming to stare, but could relish the fact that they were actually in the same room as a man who had been lost in the swamps of the Amazon, had been captured by Indians, and escaped by night, through alligator-infested waters, in a small canoe. . . . All Garlet was buzzing with the exploits of Major Fauxe, which promised to become a kind of sequel to the Weird.

He was a thin, hard-bodied, youngish man, with brown skin already scored into lines around his eyes and across his forehead; he had very bright eyes, the colour of cornflowers, and a mouth which curled up at the corners, but was firm in the way of a person who knew what he wanted, and was accustomed to have it. Yet when he smiled, he looked quite different; his blue eyes twinkled, and his lips parted to show unexpectedly uneven teeth.

It was Richard he smiled at first, while Mrs. Fauxe and Mr. Darke launched into conversation about the new stock market which was to be built at Millkennet, and Richard saw that in his tanned hands Robert Fauxe was holding the cup with curly handles, which his father had taken to Garlet Place the day before.

'Did you find this?' he asked.

'Well, no, not exactly,' said Richard. 'It was Adam's dog, Foxy, really. He went down a hole, and came up with the cup—or whatever it is—stuck over his head.'

Major Fauxe nodded.

'Then you should buy him a treat out of the money you get for it,' he said. 'It's a vegetable dish—silver—probably part of a dinner service. Of course its lid is missing, and it's in very poor condition, but the metal alone should be worth a few pounds to you, I should think.'

Not long ago, Adam would immediately have cut in with the question, 'How many?' but now he was not so interested. He only thought how absurd it was that after all these weeks of worry about pence, they should suddenly have access to pounds, when they didn't need money any more.

Richard said, 'But Major Fauxe, it isn't really ours.'

Major Fauxe shrugged his shoulders.

'It isn't anyone else's,' he replied.

'Well, thank you very much,' Richard said. 'I hadn't thought of us being allowed to keep it, or how much it was worth. When we found it I only cared because—well, if you'd had the real Communion cup to give back to the Church at Garlet, you'd have been safe for the rest of your life, and Mrs. Fauxe wouldn't have had to worry any more.'

But as he spoke, Richard saw the eyes which had been regarding him with casual friendliness, harden into a sharper awareness, and he stopped, wondering if he had said something out of place. They were disconcerting, these Fauxes, with their huge noses and bright, intelligent eyes. But Major Fauxe did not reply sharply; he put the blackened silver dish on the edge of the table, drew Richard towards him, and leaned his elbows on his knees.

'You're talking about the Weird,' he said.

'Yes.'

'You believe in it.'

'I don't know. It's different now you're back, of course, but when you were lost, we couldn't help wondering.'

Major Fauxe looked thoughtful.

'No, I suppose not,' he said. 'But it's a lot of nonsense for all that, you know—a fairy tale, in which I am unfortunately a character. I mean—just think of it. Do you honestly imagine that because a mean criminal—for that's all Lord Robert de Fauxe was—stole a cup from a church more than four hundred years ago, and a priest—who doesn't sound to me as if he was a very good Christian—cursed him for doing it, innocent people hundreds of years later would be made to suffer? Do you think our lives are ruled by such events?'

'It doesn't seem very likely,' admitted Richard, and indeed, put like that, it did not.

'I should think it doesn't,' said Robert Fauxe. 'Surely no reasonable person could believe that the Fauxes came out for the Stuarts in the Forty-Five because the Weird forced them—they did what they thought was right, and took the consequences when things went against them. And it's the same with me. When I went on that trip up the Terahucco, I knew it was dangerous, but I thought it was right for me to do it, and anyway I happen to believe that it's a poor life if you never do anything dangerous. If I hadn't come back, it would have been sad for my wife and my mother, but it wouldn't have had anything to do with the Weird. We're the ones who decide how we'll live our lives, for good or ill—nothing's decided by people cursing other people in a bad temper.' Major Fauxe paused, then suddenly he laughed, and punched Richard lightly on the shoulder. 'You're as bad as my mother,' he said. 'She believes in the Weird too. She thought we should get a bulldozer in to dig up the foundations of Fox House, just in case Lord Robert's cup should still be lying around somewhere.'

Richard could scarcely believe his ears. He spun round on his heel, and glared at Mrs. Fauxe indignantly.

'You didn't!' he burst out. 'After all you said to me in the car that night—well, really!'

Mrs. Fauxe grinned sheepishly.

'I had a moment of weakness,' she said.

And Richard saw the joke, and laughed, and winked at her, and only later wondered how he had dared.

Adam, who had been listening to Major Fauxe with an approving expression on his face, since he was saying what he had always thought about the Weird, now broke into the conversation in a piercing voice.

'Major Fauxe, will you tell us some of your adventures?'

He was impatient, because time was passing, and he wanted facts, information, so that he could tell Puss in the morning, and hold up the arithmetic lesson, and boast that he had heard it all from the Man Himself.

'Yes, I shall,' promised Robert Fauxe, 'but not today. Today I want to speak to your parents in private, if they can spare me a few minutes.'

'Certainly,' said Mr. Darke, getting up in some surprise. 'If you'll come into the sitting-room, Major Fauxe—'

Major Fauxe got up too, and followed Mr. and Mrs. Darke out of the kitchen, and for Richard it was as if the sun had gone behind a cloud. He sat down on the warm cushion of the chair the man had left, and drifted into a lovely day-dream, in which he grew up, and joined the

Scots Guards, and became an intrepid major who led dangerous expeditions up the Amazon, the Congo, the White Nile. . . . Meanwhile Anne poured more tea, while Mrs. Fauxe and David argued amicably about horses, and Adam, denied his story but not left without hope, went under the table with Foxy, to play. Ten minutes passed, twenty minutes, and the clock struck for half-past four. Five minutes after that, the three adults came out of the sitting-room; Richard, roused by Major Fauxe's voice, could see them smiling and shaking hands, through the half-open kitchen door. Scraps of conversation floated in:

'That's settled, then.'

'—Very glad indeed—'

'—Thought you'd be interested.'

Adam stuck his head out from under the table cloth and grimaced at Richard, his whole face a question mark, with eyebrows shooting up into his unruly red hair. Indeed, the whole air of the kitchen was thick with questions. But the children had to wait till the Fauxes had gone, with more handshakings and expressions of satisfaction on the door-step, before their parents came back into the kitchen.

'We're saved, it seems,' said Mr. Darke. 'Major Fauxe is leaving the Army at the end of the year, and coming back to live at Garlet Place. He wants to try his hand at farming—he has capital, but of course he has no experience. So he's asked me to go into partnership with him, working this croft, and the bigger farm he has up behind Garlet. And he says that if any of my three sons wants to be a farmer, later on, we'll find a place in the business for him too.'